A BEAUTIFUL KIND OF CRUEL

Isla March

Royston Knight Publishing
TRUTH. WIT. INK.

© 2025 Isla March
All rights reserved.
First published in the United Kingdom.

No part of this publication may be copied, reproduced, stored in a retrieval system, transmitted in any form, or by any means—electronic, mechanical, photocopying, recording, or otherwise—without the prior written permission of the author, except in the case of brief quotations embodied in critical reviews and articles.

This is a work of fiction.
All characters, names, places, events, and incidents are either products of the author's imagination or used fictitiously. Any resemblance to actual persons, living or dead, or actual events is purely coincidental. The psychological themes, emotional content, and subject matter are designed for fictional storytelling and should not be interpreted as therapeutic advice or psychological guidance.

This book is published in good faith. The author and publisher shall not be held liable for any loss, damage, or psychological disturbance allegedly arising from the content herein. Reader discretion is advised.

CONTENTS

Chapter 1	5
Chapter 2	23
Chapter 3	45
Chapter 4	65
Chapter 5	91
Chapter 6	117
Chapter 7	145
Chapter 8	173
Chapter 9	203
One year later	243

Chapter 1

The parcel arrived in early March, dropped without ceremony through the old brass letterbox, its thud absorbed by the Persian rug Vivienne had once insisted was "too good for shoes." The rug hadn't been hoovered in months. It was where Eve left everything she didn't want to deal with straight away—leaflets, charity bags, unopened bills, and on this particular morning, a brown paper package that didn't bear a return address.

She stepped over it three times before she picked it up.

It was heavier than it looked, about the size of a small hardback book, wrapped in brown Kraft paper, the edges taped with surgical neatness. Her name—*Eve Calder*—was written in ink so black and crisp it looked pressed into the surface. No first-class sticker, no date stamp, no franking. Just her name. Just here.

She didn't open it. Not yet. She placed it on the kitchen table beside her teacup and sat opposite it like it might ask her a question.

Outside, the coastal wind slapped against the windowpanes with its usual smugness. The house creaked as it always did when the damp set into the beams—like a tired body shifting under the weight of memory. Eve lit the second candle of the day, her match trembling ever so slightly before it caught.

Then she stared at the package.

Ten minutes passed.

Twenty.

She picked it up again. Turned it over.

Written across the back, in smaller handwriting but the same inky black:
"I didn't know where else to send it."

No name. No explanation.

Just that.

By the time Eve sliced the tape, her fingertips felt cold. She used the knife she normally reserved for lemon peel—slender, precise, never quite sharp enough. She cut too shallow at first, barely scratching the paper. On the second attempt, it gave way with a hiss, revealing a box lined in green felt.

Inside: a bundle of reel-to-reel tapes, stacked neatly.

Seven in total.

Each labelled by hand, not typed. The first one on top:
"V. VALE – HALFWAY HOUSE – SESSION 1 – JULY 1994"

Vivienne.

Her aunt had died two summers ago. A quiet stroke, the kind the neighbours said was "merciful." Eve hadn't cried. She hadn't attended the funeral either. They'd had an agreement, unspoken and unbroken: silence was safer.

Eve ran her finger along the handwritten label, then flipped it. On the back of the first reel, in faded biro, a second note:
"For your ears only. Do not digitise."

Something cold bloomed in her stomach. The same feeling she used to get when a camera lens refocused mid-interview, and she could tell the subject was about to confess something they'd regret.

She reached for her old reel player—dusty, buried beneath books and unopened boxes from her last flat. Plugged it in. Said a quiet, bitter prayer.

And pressed play.

The static was faint at first—white noise like rain on tin.

Then a voice: unmistakably Vivienne's. Low. Smooth. Controlled.

"Do you remember what you said to me that night, Eve?"

Eve stopped breathing.

Not *someone called Eve*. Not coincidence. Not drama.

Her.

She pressed pause. Sat back. Let the room swallow the silence that followed.

The house creaked again—this time louder, like it too had heard the voice.

The kettle boiled. She forgot she'd even turned it on.

There were seven tapes.

Each labelled with dates spanning two decades.

Eve stood up, walked to the sink, poured the boiling water away without making tea, and whispered to no one: "What the hell did I say?"

It took her five days to listen to the rest of the first tape.

She couldn't bring herself to sit through more than two or three minutes at a time. Every sentence Vivienne spoke—her rich, molasses-thick voice curling through the static—felt like a summons. A threat made softly. A recollection offered with too much precision. There was no anger in it. No cruelty. Which somehow made it worse.

On the third day, Eve dreamt of the summer Vivienne had come to stay after her mother's second breakdown. She'd been twelve. Vivienne had brought strange tea in glass jars and made her sleep with the windows open. Eve remembered her aunt standing at the end of the hallway one night, whispering something into the air, like she was coaxing the walls to forget. Or remember.

She hadn't thought about that summer in years.

And yet the moment she heard Vivienne's voice say her name aloud on tape, it returned like a slap.

On the sixth day, she made a list.

Eve Calder always made lists when panic hovered.

On the back of an old shopping receipt, she wrote:

TAPE 1

Session 1 – Mentions me by name

July 1994 – I would've been 7? No—12.

Vivienne sounds sober. Controlled. Recording alone?

Says "the girl doesn't remember." Refers to me as "the girl"?

Mentions mum. But cryptically. "Your mother was never meant to hold that kind of weight."

Ends with sound of something breaking—glass? Cup?

She put the list in the drawer with the rest of her unposted letters. Sat for a while. Looked at herself in the reflection of the oven door—warped, too tall, featureless. Then took out the second reel.

That's when she heard it.

Not Vivienne's voice this time.
Her own.

It was unmistakable.

She was younger—soft-spoken, clipped vowels, the careful way she used to mimic adults when she wanted to sound braver than she was.

The sentence was clear:

"If I tell, it'll get out. That's what you said."

Followed by a rustle.

Vivienne's voice: "It's already out, darling. You just haven't found it yet."

Then the tape clicked off, abrupt. Like the rest had been scrubbed.

Eve stood there for a full minute with the reel still spinning.

There were only five words she could say, and she said them aloud.

"Why the fuck was I recorded?"

The doorbell rang.

She jolted so hard the tape snapped clean off the spindle.

It was nearly dark. No one ever visited. The closest neighbour was a mile down the lane and blind in one eye. She hadn't ordered anything. Mara would never show up unannounced. And yet the bell rang again.

She turned off the lamp.

Moved slowly, barefoot, toward the door.

Peered through the frosted glass.

A man.

Dark coat. Clean boots. Holding a square box wrapped in waxed paper.

Eve didn't open the door. Not yet.

She spoke through it, voice low. "Who are you?"

"Leo Hartwright," he said. "I knew your aunt."

Of course he did.

She left him waiting for seven minutes. She counted.

It was just long enough to imply uncertainty, long enough to rattle someone if they were here under false pretence. Long enough to watch him shift his weight once, glance down the lane, and tap the parcel against his thigh. He didn't knock again. He just waited.

She opened the door to a slit, the chain still fastened.

He smiled—mild, unsuspicious. Not handsome in the usual way, but neat, measured. Like someone who ironed socks. His hair was the kind of brown that went mousey in certain light, and his coat looked too clean for a country road.

"I'm Eve Calder."

"I know."

He offered no hand. She liked that. He held the parcel out between them like a peace offering.

"I found something I think belongs to you."

She didn't reach for it. "Most things don't."

His smile faltered, just a fraction. "It's from the archive. Your aunt made an arrangement years ago. There are recordings—old interviews, notes, reflections, some labelled, most not. I run the cataloguing now."

"Why bring it here?"

"Because yours wasn't logged. It wasn't meant to be found."

Her jaw tensed. She didn't ask how he knew it was hers. She already suspected.

She let him in.

Not out of trust, but because instinct said: *Better to control the conversation than let it drift down the lane.*

He stepped inside carefully, like the floor might judge him. She watched his eyes flick briefly to the rug by the letterbox, the unwashed mug by the kettle, the unlit fireplace. Nothing lingered.

"I haven't had time to clean," she said flatly.

He nodded. "Neither have I."

That almost made her smile. Almost.

In the living room, she cleared books from the armchair with deliberate slowness. He didn't sit until she gestured.

He placed the waxed parcel on the coffee table, then rested his hands on his knees like a child waiting to be questioned. She sat opposite, legs folded underneath her, arms crossed. Her posture, unlike his, said: I am ready to leave the room at any moment.

Leo unwrapped the package with careful fingers. Inside: more reels. Smaller than hers. And one envelope, sealed with a red wax stamp that had been broken.

"She recorded you," he said.

Eve's stomach tightened. "I'm aware."

"No. I mean she recorded *all of you*. Your mother. Your sister. Even herself. She called it a 'mirror project'—her attempt to reflect the truth of your family through sound. She donated most of the reels to us under a pseudonym. But one set was labelled differently."

He slid the envelope toward her.

The front read:
"For when she comes looking. Not before."

"I haven't been looking," Eve said quietly.

"You came anyway."

She didn't open the envelope. Not yet.

Instead, she picked up one of the smaller reels. It was marked simply:
"E.C. - NIGHT 4 - UNFILTERED"

Unfiltered.

She stared at the word for a long time. It felt invasive, like something a voyeur would name a collection of stolen moments. She hadn't realised she'd said it aloud until Leo responded.

"She left very little unfiltered."

Eve looked up. "And you listened?"

"No," he said, and for the first time, something shifted behind his face. "Because it's my voice on some of them too."

There it was. The fracture.

He didn't elaborate.

Instead, he reached into his coat and pulled out a folded paper—thinner than the others, almost like tracing paper. He held it up.

"She drew a diagram once. A wheel. With your name at the centre. She said truth had to orbit the person who could survive it. Everyone else was just collateral."

Eve didn't move.

Leo lowered the paper. "I think you're the one she thought would survive it."

Eve let the silence bloom. Then she stood, slowly.

"I'll need time," she said. "And tea."

Leo nodded, settling back into the chair like someone who'd been invited to wait.

"I brought patience," he said. "She told me I'd need it."

The kettle shrieked louder than necessary, as if voicing everything Eve wasn't saying. She didn't silence it straight away. She let it cry out, let it echo through the bones of the house, watched Leo's silhouette from the kitchen as he stood to examine the photographs on the bookshelf without touching a single frame.

She hated how comfortable he looked.

She didn't trust people who made themselves comfortable in other people's grief.

She made the tea deliberately strong. No sugar. No milk. The way Vivienne used to drink hers—boiled until bitter, a tongue-stainer. Leo took the cup with a thank-you nod, no comment. She admired that.

They sat again. Two cups. One silence.

He broke it.

"Do you remember being recorded?"

She sipped. "Do you remember being born?"

Leo nodded, as if conceding. "Sometimes we remember what we weren't meant to. Sometimes we erase what we weren't supposed to survive."

"You speak like a therapist."

"I'm not."

"What are you?"

His eyes didn't waver. "A survivor."

It wasn't the answer she wanted, but it was the one she understood.

She opened the envelope.

Inside: a single cassette. Not a reel. A cheap plastic tape, the kind you'd find in charity shops or glove compartments. It had no label. Just a faint pencil mark: **"Eve. 2001."**

She blinked. That couldn't be right.

She was in sixth form. The year she dyed her hair black, stopped wearing dresses, and started skipping assemblies. The year she stopped trusting adults altogether. The year she broke down in front of the school nurse and never told anyone why.

She placed the tape beside her mug. Didn't touch it.

Leo watched her closely, but didn't press. He finished his tea slowly, like someone who'd been taught that silence creates its own kind of pressure.

"Who sent this?" she asked finally.

He shrugged. "It was logged by someone in the transfer department. No name. Just instructions: deliver in person. To you. Nobody else."

"And you did that? Just like that?"

"I owed her."

Vivienne.

Of course.

"What did she do for you?"

He looked out the window before answering. As if checking that no one could overhear.

"She forgave something I couldn't say out loud."

That struck her harder than she expected. She stared at him. "You knew her well, then."

"Only in fragments. I think that's how she preferred it."

Eve reached across the table and picked up the cassette. It felt too light. Too harmless. Like an object pretending not to be dangerous.

"Why now?" she asked.

Leo took a long breath.

"Because someone else is looking for the recordings. Someone who won't stop until they find them."

Her stomach turned cold.

"You think they'll come here?"

"They've already tried the archive. Twice. Called it a 'reclamation request'—said they had family rights. They didn't. We checked. Their name wasn't in her will. Or her files. Or yours."

"So who were they?"

Leo's expression sharpened slightly.

"I think that's what we're going to find out."

In the corner of the room, the old reel machine clicked back into motion.

Eve hadn't touched it.

Both of them turned to look.

The tape she thought was finished—*the first one she'd played, the one she'd stopped halfway*—was spinning again.

Vivienne's voice returned, this time clearer, more direct.

"If she's hearing this," it said, "then we've run out of safe hands."

Leo rose to his feet. Eve didn't move.

Vivienne's voice grew colder:

"She'll want the truth now. But it won't want her."

Eve didn't sleep that night.

Not properly.

She sat in the armchair long after Leo had gone, the cassette still unopened on the table, her second mug of tea long since cold. The fire remained unlit. The lights stayed low. She watched the house behave around her—walls expanding with the night chill, floorboards sighing beneath unseen weight, the occasional tick of pipes still deciding whether to give in to rust.

The tape recorder remained silent. No more tricks. No more uninvited replays.
Just that one voice, last heard hours ago, still vibrating under her skin:

"She'll want the truth now. But it won't want her."

At 2:14 a.m., she did the thing she hadn't done in a year.

She called her sister.

It rang twice, then went to voicemail.

She didn't leave a message.

Instead, she hung up and typed a message instead—deleted it. Wrote it again—deleted that too.

In the end, she sent:

"**Mara. Something's come up. I might need you here. Please don't tell anyone I asked.**"

No kiss. No explanation.

Just that.

And she turned her phone off immediately after sending it.

By morning, the house had shifted into a new kind of silence. A thinner one. Like something had been bled out.

Eve wrapped the tape in kitchen towel and placed it in a Tupperware box in the freezer. She didn't want it in the room. Not yet. Not after what Vivienne had said. She wasn't being superstitious. She was being strategic. She didn't want it to *warm*.

When she opened the back door, the wind hit her face like a wet hand. Spring was fighting its way in, but it hadn't won yet. The garden was mostly untended—overgrown rosemary, dried out soil, a birdbath half full of moss. Vivienne used to say that rosemary was good for memory.

Eve considered yanking the whole thing out.

By mid-morning, the house was too quiet again.

So she did what she always did when something needed distracting: she cleaned.

She stripped the bed. Washed the tea mugs. Vacuumed the rug Vivienne had once sworn was from Marrakesh (though it had a Made in Derbyshire label stitched into the fringe). She rearranged the bookshelf by author's first name. Alphabetical. She opened every window in the house and let the air in, even though it stung.

And when she finally sat back down, hands raw from bleach, there was a text waiting.

Mara:
"I'll be there by nightfall. You'd better not be dead or dramatic."

It was the closest thing to affection Mara had ever sent by phone.

At 5:41 p.m., the power went out.

No warning. No flickering. Just *gone*.

The house fell immediately into a silence so total it made her ears ring.

Eve didn't move straight away.

She waited to see if it would come back.

When it didn't, she stood—calm, controlled—and fetched the torch from the kitchen drawer, the one Vivienne had always insisted stay fully charged and reachable.

As she turned it on, something caught her eye.

In the living room, on the coffee table where she'd left the tapes:

One was missing.

She hadn't played it. She hadn't touched it.

But the fourth reel in the stack—the one marked **"Felix – Intake Session – 2009"**—was no longer there.

And she was very, very sure it had been.

She searched the room, the floor, the shelf. Nothing.

Then she noticed something else.

The rug by the front door—her mess rug, the one no one else would notice—had a fresh footprint in the edge dust.

Too large for hers.

Too dry for Leo's.

Too recent to be old.

Eve stood very still. The torch in her hand hummed faintly.

Outside, somewhere in the field beyond the garden wall, a car engine coughed into motion.

Then drove away.

Chapter 2

Mara arrived just after midnight, headlights sweeping across the hedgerow like a searchlight in reverse. Eve stood by the upstairs window, light off, watching the little silver car pull up onto the gravel, engine ticking as it cooled. Mara didn't get out immediately. She sat for a moment, then finally opened the door and emerged with a coat far too thin for March, a half-empty bottle of vitamin water, and a look that screamed, *If I'm here, someone better be dying.*

Eve met her at the door with no hug.

"You came."

Mara pushed past her, sniffed the hallway like it might offend her. "If this turns out to be about a bad dream or one of your dead-cat moods, I swear to Christ I'll reverse out of here with the door still open."

Eve shut the door behind them. Locked it. "Someone's been in the house."

Mara turned slowly, lips pressed thin. "Start with that next time."

They sat in the kitchen—Eve's second pot of tea of the night, Mara's third attempt at lighting a cigarette indoors before Eve finally let her crack the window.

"You're sure?" Mara asked.

"Yes."

"Not just forgetful? You're a bit—well—you go places sometimes."

Eve didn't bite. "A reel's gone. One labelled with Felix's name."

Mara frowned. "Felix? Your Felix?"

"Don't call him that."

"Alright. The Felix you married, then divorced without explanation and haven't spoken of since. That Felix."

Eve poured the tea.

Mara softened, just slightly. "So what are these tapes? Like... voicemails?"

"Recordings. Audio reels. Left by Vivienne."

"Of course they were."

Mara ran a hand through her fringe, blew smoke out the window. "God, you always said she was odd. But this is another level. It's like a crime podcast waiting to happen."

"She recorded all of us."

"Us?"

"You. Me. Mum. Him."

Mara's cigarette paused halfway to her mouth. "What?"

Eve met her gaze. "You're on one too. You haven't heard it yet."

They didn't speak for a moment.

The wind rattled the latch above the Aga. Something creaked upstairs.

"Did you call the police?" Mara finally asked.

Eve shook her head. "What would I say? That a man showed up with tapes from our dead aunt, then someone came and stole one during a blackout I can't prove happened because the power came back on ten minutes later?"

"Point taken."

Mara took another drag. "So what now?"

"I want to listen. To all of them."

"And you want me here why? Moral support?"

"No," Eve said, slowly. "Because you were part of it too. You just don't remember."

Mara flinched—not visibly, but Eve saw the edge in her cheek tighten.

"I don't remember much from back then," Mara muttered. "And frankly, I'm not keen to start."

Eve stood and opened the freezer.

Pulled out the Tupperware.

Set it on the table between them.

Mara stared. "Please tell me that's not soup."

Eve opened the lid and revealed the cassette. Still wrapped. Still labelled: **Eve. 2001.**

"What the hell's on that?" Mara asked.

"I don't know."

"And you froze it?"

"I didn't want it near me until you arrived."

"That is not a comforting sentence."

Eve held her sister's gaze. "You want the truth?"

Mara leaned back. "I think I came for it, didn't I?"

Outside, the wind dropped.

The house stilled again, as if listening.

Mara reached forward, picked up the cassette, turned it over. "I'll need wine."

"There's red in the pantry. Don't touch the one with the wax seal."

"Why?"

"It's labelled 'Don't open unless you've bled.'"

Mara blinked.

"Vivienne's idea of humour," Eve added.

Mara stood, laughing despite herself. "God, I missed you."

"You left."

"You pushed."

They looked at each other.

No more was said.

But something old shifted in the silence.

Not forgiveness. Not yet.

Recognition.

The kind that comes before the storm.

The tape clicked into the old Walkman with a faint, familiar rattle.

Eve had found it under a pile of garden gloves and a dead torch in the pantry drawer—the Walkman, that is. She hadn't used it since university. The batteries were half-corroded, but she cleaned them with vinegar and hope. Now it sat between them on the table, tethered to two battered foam headphones they took turns with like a childhood secret.

Mara poured the wine. No glasses—just mugs. The moment didn't call for ceremony.

"Ready?" Eve asked.

"No," Mara replied. "But hit play anyway."

The tape began with silence. Not blankness, but a living sort of hush—background noise, the hum of a room, distant birdsong, the light shudder of someone breathing through their nose.

Then a voice.

Not Vivienne's. Not theirs.

Male.

Muffled. Detached.

"Is this recording?"

A brief pause.

Then the unmistakable sound of Eve's voice—aged seventeen.

"It is. Just talk. You promised you would."

Mara glanced up sharply. Eve looked like she'd been slapped.

The man's voice again. Still unclear. **"You said you wouldn't keep it."**

"I lied."

The tape crackled. A scrape. A sigh.

Then the man again, softer. Regret threaded through his vowels like a pulled stitch.

"What if they find this?"

"Then they'll know it wasn't all me."

Another pause.

"I loved you, Eve."

Silence.

Then Eve's younger voice, quieter than before:

"That's why it was easy."

Mara hit stop.

Hard.

The Walkman made an ugly mechanical choke as the tape halted.

They sat in silence. Neither of them breathed properly.

Finally, Mara said, "Was that him?"

Eve nodded.

Mara rubbed her face with both hands. "Jesus Christ."

Eve stared at the Walkman like it might come alive and bite her.

"He said that to you?"

"Yes."

"And you recorded it?"

"I did."

Mara stared. "But... why?"

Eve didn't answer.

Because the truth was: she didn't remember doing it.

Not fully.

Fragments, yes. The weight of it. The fear. The deliberate way she'd set the tape rolling before he came round that night.

But the words?

They hit her now like strangers.

And worse—**she sounded cold.** Detached. Almost pleased.

What kind of girl had she been?

Mara stood up, pacing.

"This wasn't just a weird Vivienne project, was it? This goes back further."

Eve nodded, slowly.

"She kept them for a reason," Mara muttered.

"She kept *me* for a reason."

"You think she knew what happened?"

"I think she *heard* what happened."

They both went still.

Eve pulled the tape from the Walkman, cradling it in her palm.

"She was recording more than truth. She was building an alibi."

"For who?"

"I don't know."

There was a knock at the window.

Both women froze.

Not the door.

The window.

Kitchen. Side pane. No porchlight.

Mara looked at Eve. "You expecting someone else?"

"No."

The knock came again. Three short taps.

Not urgent. Just *present*.

Eve rose first.

She moved slowly to the window and drew back the curtain a fraction.

A face looked back.

Not Leo.

Not a stranger.

A woman—mid-fifties, angular, with the kind of eyes that belonged in a courtroom.

She held up a plastic sleeve with a single reel inside. Pressed it to the glass.

Written on the reel in smeared marker:

"CALDER – UNAUTHORISED COPY – 1 of 3"

Eve didn't open the window.

She stared at the woman, who stared right back.

Then the woman smiled.

Not kindly.

Knowingly.

And walked away.

By the time Eve unlatched the door and made it to the front garden, the woman was gone.

No footprints on the gravel. No sound of a car starting. Just the wind curling around the hedges like it knew something she didn't.

Eve stood at the gate in her socks, the cold seeping into her arches. The lane ahead was empty, save for the twitch of an old curtain across the road—a house that had been empty for three years.

Mara followed, coatless and annoyed.

"Tell me I didn't just see that."

"You did."

"Who the hell was she?"

"No idea. But she had a reel."

Mara ran her fingers through her hair. "Great. First a mysterious man with tapes, now a strange woman doing late-night window theatre. You've really let this place become a lighthouse for the mentally unwell."

Eve ignored her. She scanned the drive for tyre tracks. Nothing. Whoever it was hadn't parked. Which meant they'd walked. Which meant—

She turned sharply toward the back of the property.

"The field," she said.

"What field?"

But Eve was already moving.

Behind the house, the land dropped into a shallow incline, then rose again in a long stretch of grazing pasture. Vivienne used to call it "the vale"—her little joke. No one knew whether she meant valley or some private pun. Eve hadn't set foot in it since the funeral. The grass was high now, brittle at the tips. Somewhere to the left, an old wheelbarrow rusted into itself.

Mara caught up. "You're not going to find her in the dark."

"She wanted me to see the reel."

"So why not just give it to you?"

Eve stopped.

That was a good question.

She turned back to the house slowly, pulse tightening in her wrists.

"She didn't want to hand it over," she said. "She wanted me to *know* it existed."

Mara stared at her.

"Vivienne always said there's a difference between truth and proof," Eve added.

Mara crossed her arms. "And what's that supposed to mean?"

"It means she thought knowing was more dangerous than showing."

Back inside, Eve poured whisky into the mugs that had once held tea. Mara didn't argue. They drank in silence, the house creaking around them, the old floor heating up again beneath their feet.

"I want to check something," Eve said, standing.

She disappeared into the small spare room Vivienne had once used for drying herbs and reading esoteric books with unpronounceable titles. The room now held three filing cabinets and an old dresser. All locked. Except one.

Inside, Eve dug through old notebooks, receipts, yellowing newspapers.

She found it at the bottom—a black leatherette address book with half the pages stuck together from damp.

She flicked through until she found a name she half-remembered:

Clara Lynes – Herne Hollow Archive

And underneath it, in Vivienne's handwriting:

"DO NOT TRUST. But keep close."

Eve took the book back to the kitchen and showed Mara.

"That woman," she said. "I think that was Clara."

"Vivienne said not to trust her."

"She also said to keep her close."

"Well, that's a bloody mixed message."

"No. That's Vivienne."

Mara took the whisky and drained it. "So what's the plan now? You gonna call her?"

"I'm going to listen to the rest of the Eve 2001 tape. Then I'm going to call Leo."

Mara raised an eyebrow. "Why him?"

"Because he's the only one who's lied to me gently."

Mara smirked. "A beautiful kind of cruel, you mean?"

Eve looked up sharply.

Mara blinked. "What?"

"Say that again."

"I said—he lies gently. A beautiful kind of cruel. Like all men who think they're the exception."

But Eve wasn't listening.

Her mind had already dropped the thought into a much deeper well.

A memory rising like vapour. A phrase.

A voice from long ago, on a different tape.

One she hadn't listened to yet.

One she didn't even know she still had.

Leo Hartwright never liked trains.

He didn't mind the movement, or the brief illusion of anonymity, or even the rhythmic announcements that gave everything a sense of schedule. What unsettled him was the way time bent in their carriages. You could board a train as one person and disembark as someone else entirely. Just ask anyone who's ever been followed.

He sat facing backwards, deliberately, watching the landscape recede. Watching Herne Hollow disappear behind him like a secret he should never have reopened.

The folder on his lap was unmarked. Just one envelope inside.

He hadn't opened it.

Vivienne's instructions had been specific.

"If she plays Tape 3 first, don't interfere."
"If she plays Tape 1, stay close."
"If Clara reaches her before you, run."

Vivienne had been many things. A dramatist. A hoarder of private pain. A woman who knew how to disguise warnings as riddles. But she was rarely wrong.

Clara Lynes reaching Eve this early? That was a problem.

The train jolted slightly as it moved out of Dorset and into Devon. Leo didn't know where he was going yet. He only knew he needed to stay mobile. Off-grid. Out of any traceable place where the Hollow's current board could reach him.

Vivienne had warned him that Clara was still watching the archives. That she never stopped watching.

The last time he saw Clara, she'd offered him lemon cake laced with something that gave him nightmares for a week.

She'd smiled when he vomited on her porch.

"Cleansing," she'd said.
"You can't keep secrets and a stomach."

That was fifteen years ago.

He still remembered the taste.

Leo turned the envelope in his hands again. It had Vivienne's old wax seal — the crescent moon she used when she wanted someone to take her seriously.

Inside, there was said to be one photograph, one transcript, and a code word.

He didn't want to know what the code word unlocked.

He already knew the photo would show Eve. Young. Maybe unaware. Maybe not.

Vivienne had loved her in the most dangerous way: protectively.

And when Vivienne felt protective, she documented everything.

Sometimes to preserve.

Sometimes to bury.

His phone buzzed once in his coat pocket.

Unknown number.

He let it ring out.

Then another message came through.

A single text. No name.

"She's in. The house gave her Tape 4."

Leo stared at the screen, then typed back:

"Too early. That one's not safe."

No reply.

He sat still for a long time.

The train's engine hummed beneath him, indifferent.

He tapped the envelope against his knee, listening to the muted sound it made. Like something alive had curled up inside and stopped moving.

When the train pulled into the next station, Leo stood and stepped onto the platform without hesitation.

No destination.

Just movement.

The kind of movement you make when you're too close to the centre of something old. Something cracked.

And something about to detonate.

Eve couldn't sleep.

Not from fear—at least, not the kind that scrapes at the inside of your ribs. This was the quieter sort. The kind that curls up beside you in bed like a cat and waits for you to move first. The kind that smells like lavender and old wood. The kind that says, *something's already been taken from you, you just haven't noticed what yet.*

Downstairs, Mara had finally passed out on the sofa, glass of wine half-full and still warming beside her thigh. She'd made a few sarcastic remarks about the tapes, joked about Vivienne being "witchy meets MI5", then, once the second bottle kicked in, she'd gone quiet.

It was Mara's silence that always unnerved Eve. Not the shouting. The stillness.

Eve padded barefoot to the spare room, slid the drawer open, and took out the last reel she hadn't dared to touch.

Tape 4.

The one the house had restarted on its own.

The one that had Vivienne's voice warning, *"She'll want the truth now. But it won't want her."*

She turned the reel in her hands. It felt heavier than the others. Unbalanced. Like it contained more than sound.

And it did.

Because tucked behind the reel, pressed almost invisibly against the cardboard backing of the box, was a sheet of paper.

A transcript.

Typed.

Dated 2006.

INTERVIEWER: V.V.
SUBJECT: FELIX M.
LOCATION: PRIVATE HOUSE, NOT DISCLOSED
PERMISSION: UNCONFIRMED / COERCED
START OF RECORDING: 01:12:04

> **VV:** You're certain she never told anyone?
> **FM:** Yes. I think she knew not to.
> **VV:** Because she was protecting you?
> **FM:** No. Because she was protecting herself.
> **VV:** And were you a danger to her?
> **FM:** Not at first.

Eve sat down.

Very carefully.

She read the transcript through twice. It wasn't long. Most of it was blacked out—Vivienne had redacted her own copy. But what remained sent something cold and steady down Eve's spine.

The voice she'd heard on the 2001 tape—Felix's—was here too.

But different.

Not performative. Not pleading.

Just tired.

Too tired.

And *honest*.

He had told Vivienne things Eve didn't know. Things he shouldn't have said to anyone. And Vivienne had *recorded it*.

She'd had his confession, in pieces, all this time.

And she'd kept it *from her*.

Eve placed the transcript beside the reel and stood.

Her reflection in the glass of the framed map on the wall startled her. Not because it looked different, but because it didn't.

She hadn't changed.

Not in the ways that counted.

She was still the same girl sitting at the edge of someone else's apology, wondering if she was allowed to feel angry. Still the girl who had to *document everything*, just to believe it happened.

She walked to the window and opened it wide.

Cold air surged in, raising goosebumps up her arms.

Out in the distance, near the edge of the field, a faint orange glow flickered.

A fire?

No.

A cigarette.

And beside it—she could just about make out the silhouette—**the woman from the window**.

Standing still. Facing the house.

Watching.

Eve didn't move.

She let herself be seen.

Fully. Clearly.

Then she shut the window again, quietly.

No panic. No outburst.

She returned to the reel, loaded it onto the machine, and pressed play.

Vivienne's voice returned, smooth as smoke:

"If she's hearing this, then I didn't get to her in time. But maybe you can, Clara. Maybe you'll explain what I couldn't. That truth isn't redemption. It's decay."

The recording stopped.

No click. No wind-down.

Just silence.

Eve exhaled slowly.

Then whispered into the air:

"I'm not decaying. I'm waking up."

Chapter 3

By the time Mara woke up, Eve had already scrubbed the transcript clean.

Not destroyed—just altered. She'd boiled a kettle, soaked the paper in steam, then peeled away the redacted tape layer by layer with a scalpel from the emergency first aid kit. It wasn't perfect, but the effort made the point: she wasn't interested in guessing anymore.

She was done being managed by omission.

Mara squinted into the light of the kitchen like a hungover mole emerging from hibernation.

"You're making coffee?" she croaked.

"I made notes," Eve replied. "You're going to read them."

"That's not remotely the same thing."

"Black or milk?"

"IV drip, if available."

Mara sat, curled up in the threadbare armchair Vivienne had once declared "psychically heavy." She looked like she was trying to remember whether coming here had been her idea or a mistake. Her hair stuck out in odd angles and there was a faint wine smear at the corner of her mouth.

Eve handed her a strong coffee and the page she'd reconstructed.

Mara blinked. Read.

Then looked up, horrified.

"He *said* this? Out loud? To Vivienne?"

Eve nodded. "On tape. With timecodes. He gave her details."

Mara stared at the transcript again.

Not at first.

"Jesus," she whispered.

"That's the moment it turned, I think. That sentence."

Mara let the page fall into her lap. "You've never told me what happened between you and Felix. Not properly."

"Would it have changed anything if I had?"

"It would've made me hate him sooner."

They didn't speak for a while.

There was no need. The thing between them—the bruised, threadbare sibling bond—was slowly tightening. Not back to what it was, but into something more weathered. Something honest.

"You know," Mara said eventually, "this has the feel of one of those podcasts where you find out everyone's been dead for six years."

Eve gave her a flat look.

"I'm just saying. It's got *atmosphere*."

"That's not the word I'd use."

"What would you call it?"

Eve paused.

"Loaded."

They agreed to split the remaining reels that morning. Mara would take the ones without names. Eve would start with the final one: **Tape 7**, unlabelled, unnumbered, found face down at the bottom of the original parcel.

It had no markings. No tape code. No note.

Just a small, pressed flower taped to the case.

Forget-me-not.

Vivienne's favourite.

The kind of thing she used to leave in recipe books, or tucked into the edge of mirrors.

The kind of thing that always meant: *I remembered. Even if you didn't.*

Eve placed the tape into the machine.

Pressed play.

Nothing.

She fast-forwarded. Rewound. Pressed again.

Still nothing.

Then—faintly—at the fifteen-minute mark:

A voice.

But it wasn't Vivienne.

It was male.

British, older, clipped vowels.

"This is Dr John Vale. Audio log fourteen. Subject: Victoria Calder, age 29. Current status: withheld."

Eve's stomach turned.

Vale.

As in Vivienne *Vale*?

She froze.

Mara looked up from across the room. "What is it?"

Eve didn't answer.

She played the voice again.

"Audio log fourteen. Subject: Victoria Calder…"

Victoria.

Not *Vivienne*?

Not *Eve*?

No.

Their mother.

Eve stopped the tape.

Looked over at her sister.

And said, with absolute clarity:

"Mum was one of them."

Mara dropped her coffee.

The mug shattered on the flagstone floor, scattering shards and streaks of black liquid across the grouting, but neither sister flinched. The tape continued to turn—soft clicks, gentle hisses—as if it hadn't just redefined the entire terrain of their childhood.

"Mum," Mara whispered.

Eve sat very still. "Victoria Calder. Subject file. Age 29."

Mara was already shaking her head. "No. No, that's not possible."

"She had us young."

"But she wasn't—she wasn't mentally ill. She was just... complicated."

"She was institutionalised, Mara."

"Once. For a *nervous breakdown*. Not—whatever this is."

Eve rewound the tape to just before the voice. Let it play again.

"Subject: Victoria Calder. Status: Withheld."

That word. *Withheld*. It wasn't clinical. It was deliberate.

"I want to know what that means," Eve said. "What it meant. Withheld from what? From who?"

Mara crouched to pick up the shards of her cup, moving as though sleepwalking. "You think she was part of a study?"

"I think she was the study."

"But why would Vivienne have it? Why would she keep that?"

Eve looked at her sister. "Because Vivienne wasn't just eccentric. She was complicit."

They spent the next hour combing the back of every reel case, journal spine, and box lid for the name Vale. Dr John Vale. Nothing. But in one of Vivienne's old filing drawers—stuffed with dried petals and newspaper clippings and postcards from places she never visited—Mara found a sheet of headed paper, browned at the edges.

The letterhead read:

Herne Hollow Institute for Emotional Science and Subconscious Research
Founder: Dr J. Vale

Beneath it, a short letter in Vivienne's handwriting:

> "They said she was dangerous to herself. They never said what she *knew*. They used her to build the model. She never stood a chance, did she?"
>
> *"Protect the daughters. The framework's already in them."*

Mara read it twice.

Then she sat down. Hard.

"I can't breathe."

Eve knelt in front of her, took the letter gently from her hands. "She was in a programme, Mara. Before us. Maybe before she even met Dad. And they didn't just drug her or observe her."

"They *designed* her."

"And then she had us."

The silence that followed was no longer peaceful. It was procedural. Like someone had pulled the air out of the room and replaced it with the weight of something inherited.

Mara laughed suddenly—sharp, humourless. "No wonder she never hugged anyone."

"She hugged you."

"She squeezed."

Eve cracked a ghost of a smile. "That's still hugging."

"Not when it feels like containment."

They heard the front gate open.

Not slam.

Just... open.

Mara stood.

Eve grabbed the poker from the fireplace.

Mara raised an eyebrow. "Seriously?"

"I've watched enough women in documentaries *not* grab the poker."

They moved together—quiet, tense, close.

At the window, they saw her.

Clara Lynes.

Again.

This time in daylight.

And this time, she had someone with her.

A girl. Maybe sixteen. Pale. Thin. Dressed in layers too large for her.

Neither of them smiled.

Neither of them knocked.

They simply waited.

Eve opened the door.

Before she could speak, Clara held up a reel.

"This one's mine," she said. "But it speaks about you."

Eve's voice came out flat. "You keep breaking into my life."

Clara smiled, gently. "Only because yours keeps leaking into mine."

She turned to the girl beside her.

"This is Flora."

The girl didn't look up.

"She's yours too."

Eve stared at the girl.

Not because she recognised her—she didn't. But because something in her chest clenched. A tightening that wasn't fear or confusion or even recognition. It was older than that. Like the first few seconds of vertigo when standing near a ledge, knowing instinctively that the fall isn't the danger—it's the possibility you might jump.

Flora said nothing.

Didn't meet Eve's eyes.

Didn't smile.

She looked like a child who'd been taught that safety depended on silence.

Mara, ever the mouthpiece, stepped forward. "Let's try this again—who the *fuck* are you and why are you bringing lost teenagers to our house?"

Clara didn't blink. "I told you. Her name is Flora. She's part of what your aunt began. What your mother survived. And what Eve has now inherited."

Eve's fingers twitched around the doorframe. "Stop speaking in riddles."

"I'm not. You just haven't caught up yet."

"I will if you start telling the truth."

Clara sighed, slow and patient. "Truth doesn't arrive all at once. If it did, you'd reject it."

Mara made a strangled noise. "Are you quoting a bloody fortune cookie or just enjoying the sound of your own mystery?"

But Flora finally looked up.

One glance. Direct.

Right at Eve.

And said, very softly:

"You were on the tape they played us."

Eve felt her entire body still.

"What tape?"

Flora bit her lip. "It was old. You were younger. Your voice was different. You sounded like you were telling a story. But you were crying."

Mara swore under her breath.

Clara stepped in. "They used her as proof of concept. For 'post-integration empathy retention'."

"What the *hell* does that mean?"

Clara's face didn't change. "It means Vivienne's research wasn't theoretical. It was implemented. And Flora was one of the children who came through the trial group."

Eve's voice cracked. "Trial for *what*?"

Clara finally said it.

"Behavioural grafting. Emotional re-encoding. The Calder Framework."

Flora shifted slightly, drawing her sleeves over her wrists.

"You were like... the example. Like, the one who *didn't* break."

Eve swallowed hard. "You make it sound like I passed some test."

"You did."

Clara stepped forward, more gently now.

"And now you have to decide if you'll dismantle it, or let it keep running."

Mara cut in, eyes wide. "No. Sorry. What *running*? Where? Who's running it?"

"Herne Hollow. The Institute. Rebranded. Sanitised. But the framework—the emotional blueprint, the recordings, the calibrations of truth and trauma—it's all still there. Just cleaner."

"Cleaner," Mara said, horrified.

Clara looked down. "More clinical. Less bruising. More data."

Eve turned her gaze to Flora.

"What do you remember?"

Flora shrugged. "Mostly rules. Quiet rooms. Scripts. A tape recorder in every corner."

Mara whispered, "Christ."

Eve said nothing.

Because she remembered.

The same rooms. The same rules.

The exact placement of the recorder on the shelf.

She had thought it was therapy.

She had thought *everything* had been therapy.

She hadn't realised it was training.

Clara placed the reel down gently on the hallway table.

"This one has your father on it."

Mara blinked. "Our father?"

"You don't remember him clearly, do you?"

"Of course we do."

Clara just nodded.

"As I said. Truth arrives in layers."

Flora looked back to Eve.

"I wanted to meet you," she said quietly. "Just to know you were real."

And with that, she stepped back out into the fading daylight and followed Clara down the garden path.

No goodbyes.

No requests.

Just the quiet departure of someone who'd delivered something heavy and couldn't afford to carry more.

Eve closed the door.

And whispered to Mara:

"What if I was never meant to forget?"

The reel sat on the table like a dare.

Eve hadn't touched it since Clara placed it down—flat, casual, like it didn't weigh more than all the air in the room. But it did. There was something about a father's voice, especially when it had been missing for over twenty years, that turned even the strongest stomach into a fist.

Mara stared at it.

"You ever remember him saying anything worth recording?"

Eve shook her head. "No."

"I remember his shoes," Mara said suddenly. "Weird, right? Not his voice. Not his face. Just the sound of his shoes on the stairs. Heavy. Like he was always angry even when he wasn't."

Eve didn't respond. She was already loading the reel onto the player.

No hesitations.

Just inevitability.

It started with static.

Then breathing. Shallow. Fast. The kind of breathing that belonged to someone trying not to lose it completely.

And then: a voice.

Male. Ragged. Broken in strange places.

"If this is being archived, I want to be clear. I never agreed to the final phase."

Mara paled.

"I told her—Vivienne—I told her this wasn't what we'd said. It wasn't the design. I was meant to observe. To write. That was it."

Pause.

"She used them. Our daughters. She said it was ethical because they were born into it. No interference. No... outside contamination. But you can't call it clean just because the petri dish has your name on it."

Silence.

"Victoria didn't even know. Not fully. She thought she was participating. She didn't realise she *was* the prototype."

Eve's whole body went still.

She could feel Mara breathing behind her—sharp, shallow gasps. The kind she used to get in PE when her asthma hadn't been properly diagnosed.

They listened.

"I can't do this anymore. I've documented everything I can. The reflex mapping, the behavioural graft attempts, the failed reversions... but they keep watching the girls. Not interfering. Just waiting. And I know what they're waiting *for*."

"They're waiting to see who breaks first."

A longer pause this time. More rattling breath.

"If you find this, and you're one of them, then burn it. Burn this whole house of cards. But if you're them—if you're Eve or Mara—then listen to me."

"You weren't experiments. You were daughters. I tried. I did. But I was weak. And your mother was rewritten before you were even born."

"I'm sorry."

Click.

The tape ended.

Eve didn't move.

Mara sank to the floor, arms folded over her knees, forehead pressed against her sleeves.

For once, no sarcasm.

Just grief. Stale, unlabelled grief from a father they had buried in pieces long before his actual funeral.

Eve stared at the machine. Her hand hovered over the rewind button, then dropped.

"I think he thought he was protecting us," she said quietly.

Mara let out a laugh, brittle as glass. "Well, he did a shit job."

"He was scared of Vivienne."

"Everyone was scared of Vivienne."

"Even Vivienne."

They sat like that for a long time.

No talking. Just shared silence. A mutual kind of damage.

Outside, the clouds gathered fast—coastal weather pulling in, sudden and grey.

Eve stood and closed the curtains.

"I want to know what he meant," she said. "Final phase. What was it?"

Mara wiped her eyes. "I don't know. But I've got a bad feeling."

Eve nodded.

Then added, almost absently:

"I think I'm starting to remember things I didn't live."

The package came in silence.

No postmark. No courier. No knock.

Just there—on the doorstep—when Mara opened the front door to smoke and found the pale brown jiffy bag folded neatly against the mat like someone had knelt to place it.

She didn't call Eve.

She brought it inside, peeled the flap, and tipped the contents onto the hallway table: one tape, no label, no markings—and a photograph.

The photo wasn't old.

It was *yesterday*.

Taken through a long lens.

It showed Eve, standing by the back window, the curtains parted just enough to let in the late-afternoon light. Her face angled down, her fingers pressed against the glass.

Watching something.

Or being watched.

Mara dropped the photo like it burned.

"Eve?"

No answer.

She walked through the house—checked the kitchen, the lounge, the library room, the back garden. Nothing. No Eve. Just half-drunk tea and the subtle panic of things left in motion.

Her chest tightened.

She ran upstairs.

Eve wasn't in the bathroom. Not the bedrooms.

But the attic door was open.

A single ladder pulled down.

Eve was up there.
Cross-legged.
Surrounded by boxes marked with numbers, not names.
Boxes she'd never seen before.

She turned her head slowly as Mara climbed through.

"They were here all along," Eve said.

"In the attic?"

"In the house. Under the insulation. Behind the support beams. Labelled 'for recovery'. I thought they were hers, but they're not. They're institutional. Coded. All of them."

Mara's mouth was dry. "How many?"

"Dozens."

"Have you—?"

"No. I only opened one."

Eve held up a folder.

It read: **PROJECT: ECHO BLOOM / PHASE THREE / TEST GROUP CALDER**

Underneath that:
"Subject 002 – Sibling Graft Overlap – Initial Integrity: Weak"

Mara blinked. "Wait… *sibling*?"

Eve nodded. "They mapped our interactions. Every fight. Every moment of compliance or rebellion. They built templates off of us."

Mara swallowed. "What for?"

Eve opened the folder and turned it around.

The first page was a set of graphs.

Emotional peaks. Cognitive dips.

Handwritten along the bottom:
"Flora shows high mimicry of E. Calder, but low adaptability. Requires reconditioning."

Mara stepped back. "They were using us to *programme* her?"

Eve's voice was soft. "Not just her."

They descended the ladder in silence, each carrying a file.

The photo still sat on the table.

Eve picked it up. Turned it over.

In tiny, deliberate writing:

"You are already inside the final phase."

Mara's phone buzzed from the other room.

One text.

Unknown number.

"Stop listening. Or we'll turn the sound off."

Chapter 4

There was a saying Vivienne used to mutter when she thought no one was listening:

"They don't bury truth. They plant it."

Eve had never understood it as a child—just another one of her aunt's cryptic murmurs, filed away alongside odd rituals and herbal poultices that smelled of mould and regret. But now, standing in the hallway with the photograph in one hand and an anonymous threat in the other, she began to see it differently.

Planted truth doesn't disappear.
It waits.
It grows in the dark.
And then, when it's ready, it pushes its way into the light—whether or not you've made room for it.

She placed the reel with her father's voice back in its box. The photo followed it, slipped between the cardboard and the plastic lid like a dead leaf pressed into a novel. She didn't want to see it again. Not yet. Maybe not ever. But she couldn't throw it away.

Mara hovered nearby, silent, pale, arms folded tightly across her chest.

"Do you believe it?" Eve asked, voice low.

"The message?"

"The whole thing. That we're somehow... part of it. Carriers. Echoes. Whatever Flora and Clara think we are."

Mara let out a breath that wasn't quite a laugh. "I don't know what I believe. But I know someone sent a photo of you from outside the house and followed it with a threat. That's not metaphor."

Eve nodded slowly.

"They're watching," she murmured. "Still. Always."

"Then we watch back."

They didn't sleep that night.

They catalogued.

Tape by tape. Box by box. Each folder, each label, each line of handwriting was logged in a battered spiral notebook Eve had once used for shopping lists. The pen's ink started to bleed halfway through. Mara changed colours without comment.

In one folder, they found what looked like therapy notes—but the client name was listed only as **Subject B**. The notes referred to chronic auditory hallucinations, compulsive emotional looping, and "persistent mimetic transference".

"What the hell is that?" Mara asked.

Eve didn't answer.

Because she remembered.

Not clearly, not fully. But there was a session—one of the early ones, she thought, when Mum had first brought her to the institute. The walls were pale yellow. There was a red mark on the ceiling she used to count when she didn't want to speak.

And someone—**not Vivienne, never Vivienne**—had asked:

"What does it feel like when you feel someone else's feelings instead of your own?"

She hadn't known what to say.

So she'd lied.

"I don't."

At 4:47 a.m., the doorbell rang.

Mara jolted upright. Eve didn't move.

They looked at each other.

"Don't open it," Mara said.

Eve didn't.

But she walked to the window. Peered out through the curtain.

No one.

Just a single object left on the step.

A box. Plain. Shoe-sized.

She opened the door slowly, took it in with gloved hands, and brought it inside.

On the lid, one line of text, hand-inked:

"Proof is not persuasion. Use with care."

Inside: a single USB stick.

And a note.

Typed. Precise.

"Play me when you're ready to understand how they ended it the first time."

They didn't plug the USB in straight away.

It sat on the table between them like an uninvited guest, humming with the kind of potential that makes the room feel heavier just for housing it. The note beside it remained untouched. Eve had folded it in half after reading it once. Mara had read it three times and now looked like she regretted all of them.

"Why a USB?" Mara asked, voice low. "Everything else is tape. Analogue. Slow. Meant to decay. This feels... modern."

Eve nodded. "Deliberate."

"You think it's a trap?"

Eve's silence was an answer.

They took no chances.

Mara fetched her old school laptop from the boot of her car—a dusty, dented Mac that hadn't been online since she wrote her dissertation on psychotherapeutic transference. It whirred like a dying fan when it booted up, but it worked.

No Wi-Fi. No Bluetooth. No cloud backups.

They plugged the USB in.

One folder appeared.

"RECON_ECHO_ARCHIVE_FINAL"

Inside: a single video file.

No metadata. No creation date. No author.

Just a name:

"THE CLOSURE ROOM"

Eve double-clicked.

The video opened in silence.

Grainy footage. Static overlay.

A long corridor. Fluorescent lights humming The camera—handheld, unstable—moved down the hallway slowly. On either side, rooms with heavy doors. Most were closed. One was slightly ajar.

The person holding the camera didn't speak.

They reached the door. Pushed it open.

Inside: a circular room. White walls. No furniture. One overhead light.

In the centre, a girl.

Seated on the floor.

Maybe twelve years old.

Eve leaned forward.

The girl looked up at the camera.

She wasn't crying.

She wasn't speaking.

She just mouthed something—three times.

The same phrase.

The subtitles at the bottom of the screen translated it:

"I didn't mean to remember."

The screen went black.

Then a second clip began.

Same room. But older girl now. Seventeen, maybe.

Same position.

But this time, her mouth didn't move.

She stared into the camera for a full forty-two seconds before the feed cut to static.

Mara whispered, "Is that…?"

"I don't know."

"It looks like you."

"I don't think it is."

"It looks like you *now*."

Eve blinked.

Her reflection in the dark screen stared back.

The final clip began.

It was labelled: **"PROGRAM SHUTDOWN – INTERNAL FOOTAGE – VALE."**

A date flickered at the bottom. **17 October 2007.**

The scene: an office. Dimly lit. Bookshelves. Leather chair.

Dr John Vale—older now, gaunter than the voice on the earlier reel—sat behind a desk.

He stared into the lens. Then spoke.

"If this is the end of the programme, then you're too late. We already distributed it. The emotional signature of Subject E has been grafted. She's no longer necessary. But she remains... dangerous."

He leaned forward.

"Not because of what she knows. But because of what she *feels*."

He reached toward the camera.

"End it. If you still can."

Cut to black.

Mara sat back, stunned.

"They shut it down."

"No," Eve said quietly. "They pivoted. They spread it. That's what he meant by 'distributed'. He wasn't talking about files."

Mara whispered, "He meant *people*."

Eve nodded.

"They used me as a prototype. Then replicated the emotional blueprint."

"And Flora's one of the copies?"

"Not copies," Eve said. "*Echoes*."

She reached for the USB and unplugged it.

It was warm.

Almost too warm.

Mara stared at her.

"So what now?"

Eve closed the laptop and slid the USB into a tin marked *Dried Chamomile – Do Not Touch*.

She looked at her sister.

Then said softly:

"We find out who else is made of me."

Leo hadn't slept in thirty-six hours.

Not because he was avoiding it—though that was partially true—but because the idea of sleep felt absurd. Like blinking in the middle of an explosion. The train carriage he'd boarded that morning now felt like a bubble of time that had burst. The station platform where he'd stepped off hours earlier was a ghost town, and the B&B he'd checked into was run by a woman with one eye and no questions.

He appreciated both.

The envelope Vivienne had left for him sat on the small wooden desk beneath a flickering bulb. He'd carried it across two counties, three trains, and a moment of near-collapse at a service station in Wiltshire.

He had not opened it.

Until now.

The wax gave easily. Dry. Brittle. As though it, too, had waited too long.

Inside: three items.

> 1. A photograph of Eve, age eight, standing beside a woman who was *not* Victoria Calder.
>
> 2. A single page of typed notes. Confidential.
>
> 3. A name.

Leo stared at the name first.

Then looked again.

Then said aloud, "No."

He didn't say it like disbelief.

He said it like someone who's just found the ghost in the mirror isn't a ghost at all.

The notes were clearer than Vivienne's usual handwriting.

They were labelled:
Project: Threshold Bloom
Confidential Internal Addendum – Not for Archival

> *Subject E.C. demonstrates exceptional latency absorption in high-empathy environments. Emotional resonance exceeds previously recorded parameters. Notably, proximity to anomalous Subject A.L. (now withdrawn) results in exponential acceleration of graft formation and increased trauma mirroring.*
>
> *Conclusion: the original network cannot be disbanded safely. Containment through reintegration may prevent outbreak.*

Outbreak.

Leo underlined the word with his thumb as though he could wear the ink down.

This wasn't metaphor.

This wasn't poetry.

Vivienne had believed emotional contagion was real.

And Eve Calder wasn't just a patient or a subject.

She was the *origin*.

He picked up the photo again.

The woman beside young Eve had been cropped from all family records. She wasn't in any of the archive photos he'd seen. And yet here she was, smiling faintly, arm draped over Eve's shoulder like they belonged to each other.

The back of the photo had one line, scrawled in red ink:

"Find her before she finds Eve."

He turned to his laptop.

Hardwired. No Wi-Fi. Military-grade VPN that would make most digital ghosts blink.

He entered the name.

Nothing came up.

He tried the institute's old terminal codes. Cross-checked with recovered staff documents from the Hollow's 2002 wipe. Nothing.

Until he entered the name into a handwritten index file Vivienne had once slipped into his coat pocket during an argument.

Then: a match.

Name: **Anna Lynes**
Status: *Deceased (unconfirmed)*

Affiliation: **Subject Zero — Vale Prototype Phase**
Alias: "Clara"

He leaned back slowly.

"Shit."

Because Clara wasn't just a rogue archivist.

She wasn't just watching from the outside.

She had been part of the very beginning.

And now she was back.

He picked up his phone.

No signal.

He stood, went to the window, leaned out into the wet night air, and tried again.

One bar.

He typed a message to Eve.

Paused.

Deleted it.

Typed again.

"The woman calling herself Clara isn't Clara. She's Anna. The first one. The patient Vale tried to cure."

Pause.

Then:

"Don't listen to her. Don't *feel* near her. Don't let her rewrite you."

He hit send.

The message went through.

Barely.

He hoped it would arrive in time.

But the truth clawed at him as he sat in the dark:

It might already be too late.

Eve's phone buzzed once—low and brief—on the windowsill.

She picked it up instinctively, expecting Mara or perhaps Leo.

But the screen only showed a number. No name. No message preview. One unread text.

She opened it.

The woman calling herself Clara isn't Clara. She's Anna. The first one. The patient Vale tried to cure. Don't listen to her. Don't *feel* near her. Don't let her rewrite you.

Eve's throat went dry.

She stared at the words for several seconds before her thumb moved.

Deleted nothing. Replied with nothing.

Just... stared.

In the kitchen, Mara was speaking to someone on the landline—a journalist contact she knew from a guest lecture circuit, someone with soft access to private research institutions. Eve could hear her voice through the cracked door: controlled, clipped, urgent but still dressed in the affectation of academic inquiry.

Eve didn't interrupt.

She sat down in the hallway, back pressed against the wall, and stared at the empty tin where she'd hidden the USB earlier.

Anna Lynes.

Clara wasn't just a collector.
She was a *carrier*.

An original.

The *first experiment*.

And Eve had let her walk into the house, stand at the edge of the truth, and hand her a reel that might have been laced with more than memories.

She wasn't sure if she felt violated or flattered.

Maybe both.

When Mara finally ended the call, she walked back into the hallway with a look Eve didn't recognise. Not fear. Not anger. Just... coldness. A kind of internal winter.

"That was Halstrom," Mara said. "He confirmed the Hollow's records were partially digitised in 2010 under a private pharmaceutical archive. Guess where the data was sent?"

"Where?"

"A behavioural AI firm that rebranded as a wellness tech startup three years ago. Based in Oxford. Guess what they specialise in?"

"Emotion tracking?"

"Emotion *predictive modelling*. Based on inherited trauma and suggestibility patterns."

Eve stared at her. "You're saying they're still using us."

"I'm saying they never stopped."

They spread the remaining files across the lounge floor, cross-referencing the oldest tapes with Vivienne's spiral-bound index book. She hadn't written a key or glossary, but she had drawn diagrams—emotional constellations, looping arrows, timelines that didn't align.

Subject E. Subject B. Subject AL.

Then, scrawled in a corner like an afterthought:

"If Echoes trigger prematurely, containment must be familial."

Mara read it twice. "What does that mean?"

Eve didn't respond immediately.

Then:

"It means if they start remembering before the programme says they should, the only way to stop them fragmenting is by using *us*. The source."

"You're not a cure," Mara said quietly. "You're a leash."

Eve felt it like a slap.

And worse—like a confirmation.

Later, they lit a fire they didn't need just to anchor the silence.

Outside, the wind picked up again—that strange coastal howl that always seemed to say *you're not alone* in a way that didn't feel comforting.

Eve opened the final folder in the box Leo had brought.

Inside: a child's drawing.

Stick figures.

A house.

A small figure standing at the door.

Beneath it, written in thick pencil:

"She says I'm not real unless she feels me."

Mara leaned in. "Do you think Flora drew that?"

"I think," Eve whispered, "that someone *taught* her to."

Flora was waiting.

They found her sitting on the old bench at the top of the hill behind the garden wall—the one Vivienne had placed there for "weather readings," though no one ever saw her with a thermometer. She faced the sea, hood up, knees tucked beneath her coat. The wind played roughly with her hair, but she didn't seem to notice.

Eve didn't speak straight away.

She simply sat down beside her, leaving enough distance to suggest this wasn't a confrontation.

Mara stood back, arms folded. Watching.

Flora finally said, "I thought you wouldn't come."

Eve stared ahead. "I nearly didn't."

Flora nodded.

"I've been thinking," she added.

Eve waited.

"If I'm a copy," Flora said, "what happens if you break?"

Eve blinked.

It wasn't the question she was expecting.

She turned to the girl. "You're not a copy."

Flora didn't respond.

"I mean it. You're not a duplicate. You're your own person. You've had your own life. Even if you were shaped by something that came from me… it didn't erase you."

"That's not what the tapes say."

"They don't know you. They only measured you."

Flora looked up. "But if I was made from the shape of your pain... what happens if you *stop feeling it*?"

That did something to Eve.

A sharp little twist behind the ribs.

She realised what the girl was really asking.

Not about identity.

About *existence*.

"You think I'm your engine?" Eve said softly.

"I think I'm your ghost."

Mara stepped closer, but Eve held up a hand.

"No," she said. "Let me answer."

She turned back to Flora.

"I don't know what they did to you. Or how many others there are like you. But I know this: if they built you to feel what I feel, then you've already broken the system."

"Why?"

"Because you're here. Questioning it. That means it didn't hold."

Flora's eyes shimmered—but she didn't cry. Not the way children cry. Not openly. Just a quiet wetness at the corners, quickly blinked away.

"I still don't know who I am without you," she said.

Eve reached into her coat pocket.

Pulled out the folded drawing.

Held it out gently.

"I think this might help."

Flora took it.

Opened it.

Stared.

After a long moment, she whispered, "I didn't draw this."

Eve nodded.

"I know."

Down the hill, the cottage light flickered once.

Then again.

A signal.

Eve looked at Flora.

"Someone's trying to scramble you."

Flora frowned. "What do you mean?"

Eve rose to her feet.

"It means someone doesn't want you knowing who you really are."

They returned to the house in silence, but the air had shifted. Something less fragile now.

Mara met them at the door, her expression unreadable.

"There's been another message," she said.

She handed Eve a folded note.

Same typeface as before.

Same neutral paper.

But this one had no warning.

No riddles.

Just one name.

"AVA."

Beneath it:
"The one you forgot on purpose."

Eve's legs went cold.

She hadn't heard that name in decades.

Ava.

It struck like thunder—first confusion, then memory, then the echo of something much worse.

Because Ava wasn't a friend.
Or a classmate.
Or a relative.

Ava was…

No.

She couldn't say it. Not yet.

She looked at Flora.

Then at Mara.

And whispered:

"I think they left something out of the timeline."

The letter was hidden behind the fireplace brick—wrapped in oil paper, sealed with wax so aged it cracked when Eve touched it. She hadn't remembered putting it there. Hadn't remembered *ever seeing it*. But her handwriting was on the corner:

"Not to be read until she's named."

She sat at the kitchen table in silence.

Flora stood nearby, shifting from foot to foot, arms tightly folded across her chest like she already knew this wasn't going to end in comfort.

Mara watched from the doorway, holding the same stillness she always did before impact.

Eve broke the seal.

The letter was short.

No greeting.

No context.

Just six lines.

> "She was the control. Not the mistake."
> "They made her to see what broke when love wasn't offered."
> "I named her Ava because I thought it meant protection."
> "It doesn't. It means breath."
> "She stopped breathing on tape."
> "If you found this, she's trying to return."

Eve's hand trembled as she lowered the page.

Flora stepped closer. "What does it mean?"

"It means I wasn't the first," Eve whispered. "It means *someone else carried the pain before me*."

Mara's voice was quiet. "But who was Ava? A sister?"

"No," Eve said. "Worse."

She folded the paper carefully. "A clone."

Mara swore under her breath.

Flora sat down.

Eve stood, crossing to the corner cabinet—the one Vivienne had told her never to open unless the house "felt different." That was how she phrased it. Not *if you're in danger*, or *if someone comes*, but *if the house feels different*.

Tonight it did.

She opened the cabinet.

Inside: an old leather folder tied with twine. No label. Just a faint floral scent and one more forgotten relic pressed inside—a dried violet.

Eve untied it slowly.

Inside: a single VHS tape and a handwritten label.

"AVA / Trial Room Footage / Eyes Open at 9:41"

Mara stepped forward. "We don't have a player."

Eve nodded. "But Leo does."

An hour later, Eve's phone rang.

No number. Just *LEO – VOICEMAIL* appearing briefly before it cut off.

Then a text.

"Where are you? I've found her file. It's worse than we thought. Ava wasn't just one person. She was the prototype *and* the name they gave to every failed iteration."

Eve sat down slowly.

"What is it?" Mara asked.

Eve looked at her.

Then at Flora.

Then back at the letter in her lap.

"It means they didn't just test feelings."

She swallowed.

"They tested survival."

In the hallway, the lights flickered again.

Only this time—they didn't come back on.

Eve rose to her feet, calm.

"I think the power cuts are deliberate."

Mara grabbed a torch. "How?"

"They're not turning off the lights," Eve said. "They're turning off *witnesses.*"

She turned to Flora.

"Where were you born?"

Flora blinked. "What?"

"Not your birthday. Not the hospital. *Where* were you *born*?"

Flora's voice cracked.

"I don't know."

Eve nodded slowly.

"That's how they kept us all separate. We were never born into the same story."

Chapter 5

The VHS player Leo had sent arrived in a wooden crate nailed shut like it was housing something feral. It had no branding, no instructions—just a post-it note stuck to the lid in faint, ink-stained handwriting:

"DO NOT fast-forward. She breaks at 9:41."

Eve peeled the lid back slowly.

Inside: the player, bundled in cloth like contraband, and a second note tucked beneath the power cord.

"If you're watching this, lock the doors first. Memory is contagious."

They set it up in the lounge. Curtains drawn. Fire unlit. No sound but the distant groan of the sea through the chimney.

Mara fetched Flora a blanket. Not because she was cold, but because she looked like someone about to unravel.

Eve held the VHS tape like it might dissolve in her hand. The label—AVA / TRIAL ROOM FOOTAGE—stared back at her in jagged capital letters. Someone had rewritten over an older sticker beneath it. She could just about make out the words:

"Calder Iteration 1-A / Unstable."

She inserted the tape.

Pressed play.

And watched herself being born again—through someone else.

The screen showed a small white room.

Not dissimilar to the Closure Room from the USB footage—but colder somehow. No window. No clock. Just a girl, maybe nine, standing barefoot on a circle marked in red tape.

She wasn't crying.

She wasn't blinking.

She was waiting.

Off-screen, a man's voice spoke:

"Begin Observation Trial: Subject Ava. Emotional Trigger Series Three. Visual A."

A screen lowered in front of the girl.

A flickering video played—home footage. Birthday candles. A woman singing. Laughter. The girl didn't move.

Then: the sound of a scream.

Not from her.

From the tape.

The birthday party distorted into static. Then an image of a hospital corridor. A crash cart. A body under a sheet.

Ava blinked once.

Then turned toward the wall and said, quietly:

"That's not mine."

Mara flinched.

Flora gripped the edge of the blanket.

Eve said nothing.

Because her stomach had started to turn in a way she remembered. Not from fear.

From recognition.

On screen, the test continued.

Ava was given toys, food, photographs of strangers. Her responses were calm. Distant. Like someone being interviewed underwater.

At 9:41, the screen flickered.

Then froze.

A close-up.

Ava's eyes widened. Not fear. Not sadness.

Clarity.

And then, as if she were looking straight at Eve through the television:

"You were supposed to come earlier."

Eve stood abruptly.

Turned off the tape.

Mara shouted, "Wait—what was—"

"She saw me," Eve said. "On *that* tape. Fifteen years ago."

Flora whispered, "I saw that one too."

They both turned.

Flora's face was pale.

"That clip. The party. The scream. They played it for us in the Hollow. Said if we didn't cry, it meant we were integrating correctly."

Eve dropped into the nearest chair.

"She wasn't a subject. She was a warning."

Mara nodded slowly. "That's why they stopped using her."

"No," Eve whispered. "That's why they tried to *hide* her."

The lights dimmed.

Flickered once.

Came back.

A new sound: the fax machine in Vivienne's office buzzing for the first time in years.

Eve and Mara exchanged a glance.

They ran.

On the fax tray: a single sheet.

Fresh. Damp from ink.

No sender. No header.

Just four words.

Typed.

"AVA IS STILL ALIVE."

Ava is still alive.

The sentence throbbed against Eve's skin like a second pulse. Four words. Nothing more. No context, no timestamp, no indication of who had sent it or how—but the machine had printed it with the urgency of something *true*.

Mara stared at it. "This has to be a bluff."

Eve shook her head. "It's not."

"How can you be sure?"

"Because I remember her voice."

Flora sat on the bottom stair, knees drawn up to her chest. "They used her as a warning."

Eve turned. "To you?"

Flora nodded.

"She was the example of what happens when someone gets… stuck. When emotions loop. They called it 'feedback failure'. They said she couldn't hold her shape."

Mara frowned. "Hold her what?"

"Her identity," Eve whispered.

They didn't know where to begin looking.

Ava wasn't a person with records. She was a prototype, a code word, a ghost in a lab report. Eve's only connection to her was visceral—a half-memory stitched into her gut, a smell, a sensation, a look of someone else's fear reflected back like a mirror gone soft at the edges.

But Vivienne's old filing cabinet had *one* more drawer they hadn't opened.

The bottom one.

Eve had always assumed it was empty. It stuck, squeaked, and required a boot heel to open fully.

Inside: a lockbox.

Metal. Rusted.

The key had long gone missing.

So Eve used a chisel.

It cracked open with a finality that made Flora flinch.

Inside: old photos. Hospital bands. A patient admission form with most of the writing blurred from water damage—but one line was still legible.

NAME: Ava Vale

Mara blinked. "Vale?"

"Vivienne's surname," Eve said softly.

"She adopted her?"

"No. She *claimed* her."

The back of one photo had a scribbled note in Vivienne's hand:

"2nd attempt. Controlled environment. Shared affect threshold at 54%. Rejected maternal conditioning. Regressed 3 years. AV – unsustainable, but necessary."

Mara paced the room. "She was raising her?"

"Testing her," Eve corrected. "Vivienne was trying to graft emotions onto someone who couldn't hold them. She was trying to *build a conscience*."

"Jesus."

Eve turned the paper over again.

"She wasn't meant to live past the trial phase."

Mara paused. "So if she's alive... she escaped?"

Flora added quietly, "Or they let her go."

The landline rang.

All three jumped.

Mara reached it first. "Don't—"

Too late. Eve answered.

Silence on the other end.

Then: a breath.

And a voice—female, steady, like glass about to crack:

"I remember the scream now. It wasn't on the tape. It was in the room."

Eve's heart stilled.

"Ava?"

The line clicked dead.

Flora stood slowly.

"She's not a ghost."

"No," Eve whispered.

"She's the mirror."

Later that night, Mara found a page tucked into Vivienne's favourite book—*The Art of Radical Listening*.

It had a list of names.

Each with a location. A year. A three-letter code beside them.

Most were crossed out.

One wasn't.

AVA – BRYNMIRE – ECR

She brought it to Eve without a word.

Eve stared at the page, then up at her sister.

"ECR?"

Mara answered quietly.

"Echo Containment and Recovery."

They left before sunrise.

Eve packed only what she needed—Vivienne's notes, the fax, the VHS label, and the black-and-white photo of Ava with the date half-erased in the corner. Mara took the car keys without asking. Flora carried nothing but her headphones and a quiet fury that didn't suit her age.

Brynmire wasn't on any standard map.

You had to know how to find it—old Ordinance Survey overlays, stitched together with folklore and whispers. A coastal town with a dead signal. A memory sink. Vivienne used to say it was where the government buried the things it didn't want to officially forget.

They reached the turn-off just after midday.

The sign had been painted over in tar.

Eve hadn't told Leo they were going.

She couldn't risk it.

Not because she didn't trust him—but because **Ava hadn't called *him*.**

She'd called *her*.

And that meant something.

Mara glanced at her as they passed the final fence—a low iron rail almost entirely devoured by thorns.

"Are we sure we're not just chasing ghosts?"

Eve shook her head. "Ghosts don't make phone calls."

Brynmire was mostly ruins.

A seaside rehabilitation village turned memory research station turned correctional complex—though no one could say what it had been correcting.

They drove through empty streets.

Old houses stood with boarded-up windows and prayer symbols scratched into the wood. A pub named *The Quiet Anchor* had collapsed in on itself like it had grown too weary to stay upright.

Eve stopped outside the last standing building with power.

A concrete structure.

One narrow corridor visible through the glass.

No signage.

But the faint glow of a red emergency light told them it wasn't abandoned.

They went in.

The air was dry and pressurised. Flora winced as if her ears had popped. Mara reached for the knife she always kept in her boot.

No alarms.

No welcome.

Just a corridor of numbered doors.

Each with a label:

ECR-01, **ECR-02**, **ECR-03**...

Eve reached **ECR-08** before she heard it.

A voice.

Not behind the door.

In her ear.

Soft. Familiar.

"You were always the one they couldn't close."

She turned.

No one there.

Flora grabbed her hand.

"I heard it too."

Eve crouched. "What did she say to you?"

Flora swallowed. "She said... *I'm what you couldn't carry.*"

They were being spoken to in echoes.

Recorded messages tied to their movements, their memories, maybe even their *genetic patterns*.

Mara stared down the hallway.

"We're walking through a test."

Eve nodded. "One she never finished."

Door **ECR-09** was ajar.

They pushed it open together.

Inside: nothing but a mattress on the floor, a chair, and a wall covered in writing.

Scratched, not inked.

Claw marks.

Names.

Dozens of names, repeating in loops.

AVA. AVA. AVA. AVA.

But one stood out.

EVE.

Underlined.

Once.
Twice.
Three times.

And beneath it, a single sentence scratched deep enough to leave metal exposed.

"You left before I could tell you the ending."

The room wasn't cold.

It *should* have been, but it wasn't.

That's what unsettled Eve most. The radiator under the single barred window had been turned on recently—meaning someone had known they were coming. Or still *was* here. .

She stepped closer to the wall.

The scratched name—**EVE**—was slightly off-centre, as if whoever carved it wasn't quite sure where she belonged.

Mara touched the marks lightly. "This wasn't done in anger."

"No," Eve whispered. "It was done in grief."

Flora moved to the mattress. Underneath: a torn page from a book, folded tight like a keepsake. When she opened it, Eve caught her breath.

It was from *Vivienne's journal*.

The one that had supposedly burned in the house fire a year before Vivienne died.

> *"Ava continues to exhibit incompatible empathy. When shown projected loss, she dissociates. When shown real pain, she mirrors. But only Eve provokes spontaneous affective response. I believe this confirms my suspicion:*
>
> *They were never meant to be separate."*

Mara paced the room. "So what are you saying—that Ava was some kind of emotional twin?"

Eve stared at the words. "Or a vessel. A prototype designed to carry the parts of me I couldn't process."

"But why?"

Flora whispered, "To keep you clean."

Eve turned.

Flora's eyes were glassy with memory.

"They used to say that to us. That pain could be rerouted. If one girl carried enough of it, the others would stay functional. 'Clean' girls passed the trial. The rest got sent back."

"To where?" Eve asked.

Flora didn't answer.

Instead, she pointed to the chair in the corner.

Beneath it—barely visible—was a hidden latch.

Mara pulled it open.

A narrow tunnel, just wide enough for a child, descended below the floorboards.

Eve looked at Flora.

"Did you know about this?"

She shook her head.

"No. But it feels... familiar."

Eve knelt.

The tunnel smelled of salt and iron and something older—like the inside of a locked memory. She took a breath and began to crawl.

Mara followed.

Flora hesitated, then dropped in behind them.

The tunnel sloped downward for longer than it should have. Each turn tighter. Each breath more ragged. Until, at last, it opened into a wide, circular room.

A single bulb flickered.

A screen buzzed to life.

And Ava's face appeared.

Not a live feed.

A recording.

She looked older—late twenties—but there was a childlike serenity in her gaze, like someone who'd stopped time around herself.

She looked into the lens and said:

"If you've made it this far, then you've remembered enough to understand why you left me. And maybe why I let you."

Eve's chest clenched.

The recording continued.

> "They called me unstable because I kept seeing things I wasn't supposed to remember. Feelings I hadn't earned. But they weren't mine, Eve. They were yours. You were meant to grow up free of the Hollow. I was the one they filled up and broke open—again and again—so you wouldn't have to carry the weight."
>
> "But it leaked, didn't it?"
>
> "Somewhere between who I was and who you became, the rupture bled both ways."
>
> "And now... you need to know what's coming."

The screen cut to static.

Then another video began to play.

Footage of a lab—modern, white, endless glass and mirrors. A girl being strapped into a chair.

Not Ava.

Not Eve.

Flora.

Mara gasped.

Eve reached for the screen.

The girl on the tape looked seven. Maybe eight. Her eyes wide. Her hands calm. She turned to the camera.

And whispered:

"I tried to tell them. I wasn't the youngest."

Flora didn't move.

Not when her image disappeared from the screen. Not when Eve reached out to touch her. Not when Mara whispered her name like a cracked lullaby.

She stood utterly still—like she was afraid that breathing might break something.

"It was me," she said at last. Her voice was thin, stunned, but certain. "I was the control subject. Not Ava."

Mara stared. "What do you mean, control?"

Flora didn't answer directly. Instead, she walked to the far side of the chamber and placed her palm against the wall.

It hissed.

Then opened.

A second passageway, newer than the last.

Stainless steel, seamless floor. No dust. No rust. No trace of age or disuse.

Eve followed silently. Mara hesitated—then gave in to whatever pulled at her, and stepped through too.

The corridor buzzed faintly as they walked, like electricity was being fed through its bones.

"Where does this go?" Eve asked.

Flora replied without looking back.

"To the loop."

Mara frowned. "What loop?"

"The one they buried under every version of us."

They emerged into a room shaped like a hexagon.

Screens on each wall.

Beds, empty but labelled with names.

Some scratched out. Others still glowing.

Eve stepped closer.

One read:
EVE MARCH – Cleaved (Successor Route)
Another:
MARA MARCH – Partial Recoil (Inconclusive)
A third:
FLORA VALE – Reintegration Attempt Pending

Mara paled.

"They were watching us?"

Flora whispered, "No. *They were rerunning us.* Over and over until something stuck."

On the central screen, a reel began to play.

Not video. **Lives.** Snapshots of the sisters—at different ages, different places—some familiar, others impossible. A version of Eve working in a London hospital. Another tending bar in the Hebrides. A Flora with short hair and a burn on her right hand.

Mara stepped back. "These aren't memories."

"No," Eve said slowly. "They're *outcomes.*"

"They were trying to map every version of us?"

"Test them," Flora corrected. "Stress them. Fold them. And find the one that doesn't break."

She walked to a console and placed her hand against the sensor.

The system blinked red. Then green.

The floor beneath the beds hissed.

And the *loop chamber* revealed itself.

Six cryogenic pods.

Three used.

Three sealed.

Each bore a number, not a name.

Eve walked slowly to Pod 3.

Ava's body lay inside.

Unmoving.

Preserved.

The pod was labelled:
AV-3. Emotional Variant. Retrieval Suspended.

Eve's breath caught.

"She never left."

Mara stared. "But she spoke to you—called the house."

Flora nodded slowly.

"She did. From here. From the loop. Just like I did—before I was retrieved."

Eve turned.

"You were never adopted."

Flora blinked.

"You were placed."

She nodded.

"Vivienne didn't *take* me. She *recalled* me. After my loop began to corrupt."

Mara backed against the wall.

"This is insane. Are you saying none of us were real?"

"No," Eve said, touching the glass of Ava's pod.

"I think we're all too real."

"And that's what made us dangerous."

A console behind them powered up.

A voice—soft, distorted, but familiar—spoke through the room.

"Reintegration commencing. Loop AV-3 now merging with Primary Conscious. Host override in progress."

Flora stepped back.

The pod began to thaw.

Ava's eyes flicked.

Then opened.

Wide. Black. Knowing.

And locked on Eve.

Ava didn't gasp or flinch when the pod hissed open.

She simply stepped out barefoot, steam curling around her like a breath returned to its body. Her hair was damp. Her skin unnaturally smooth—like time had been vacuum-sealed. She blinked once, then twice, adjusting not to the light but to the *presence* in the room.

And her eyes—those obsidian wells—found Eve and *held* her.

Not like a sibling.

Like a mirror that had been waiting.

"You made it," Ava said softly.

Her voice was deeper than Eve remembered. Slower. Each word coated in something clinical, but aching underneath.

"I wasn't sure if you would."

Eve's mouth was dry.

"I got your message."

Ava tilted her head. "That wasn't a message. That was a *recall impulse*."

"What?"

"I didn't send it. You *heard* it. From me. But not through me."

Mara stepped forward, trying to wedge herself between them. "You're not making sense."

Ava blinked. "No. I'm finally starting to."

She looked at Flora. "You're cleaner than I expected."

Flora didn't speak.

Just trembled.

Eve turned back to Ava.

"What *are* we?"

Ava smiled.

But there was no warmth in it.

"You're the one who got away."

Mara frowned. "From what?"

Ava looked up at the screen.

The loop reel still turning—images of fire, of crying girls, of broken glass and sterile rooms and shadows with hands.

"From *us*," she whispered.

"You were the one whose emotion never collapsed. The one whose grief didn't crystallise. You weren't designed. You *occurred*."

Eve took a step back.

"You're wrong."

Ava followed.

"You were the anomaly, Eve. And they built *me* to carry you back."

The lights in the chamber dimmed.

The cryo pods behind them retracted into the floor.

From the far wall, a panel opened, revealing another door—this one lined with something softer than steel. Padded. Seamless.

Flora whispered, "The resonance room."

Ava nodded.

"They'll want to see if it still works."

Eve's breath caught.

"They?"

Ava's voice didn't change.

"The ones still watching."

Mara reached for her knife.

"Enough cryptic bullshit. What *is* this place?"

Ava turned to her, eyes narrowing.

"This is where they test the bandwidth of pain."

The room vibrated.

Slightly.

But enough that Flora covered her ears.

Ava stepped forward, her voice steady.

"I wasn't supposed to wake up. Not fully. Not before you completed your loop."

She looked at Eve.

"But something in you broke it early."

A screen above them flickered.

It now showed a live feed.

Of their arrival.

Of *themselves*, standing at the gate that morning. Three women. A car. A hesitant pause.

Eve's stomach twisted.

"We're being watched *in reverse*?"

Ava smiled.

"They're running outcomes *backwards*. Trying to identify the exact emotional rupture point."

"And what happens when they do?"

Ava's voice dropped.

"They rerun you. Until your empathy fails. Or your identity collapses. Whichever comes first."

A siren began to hum, soft at first, then louder.

Mara grabbed Eve's arm. "We need to leave. Now."

Ava shook her head.

"You can't."

Flora spoke at last.

"Yes we can."

Everyone turned.

Flora's voice had changed—hollow, but calm.

"I found the off-switch when I was six. I just didn't remember until now."

She walked to the console.

Typed something.

The siren stopped.

The screens went dark.

The resonance room door hissed shut.

Ava blinked.

"What did you do?"

Flora looked at her.

And for the first time, sounded like someone older than them all.

"I unlooped us."

Chapter 6

The sky outside Brynmire had changed.

It wasn't immediate. But when they stepped back through the last steel corridor and out into the light, the air felt *slower*. The clouds hung low, stitched into the sky with a sickly thread of colour—rose-gold bleeding into rust. Birds flew in erratic loops, chasing nothing. The sea beyond the town had pulled back as if it no longer wanted to touch the shore.

Something had *shifted*.

Eve said nothing at first.

She just stood there, letting the cold air catch in her throat like a held question.

Mara turned to Flora. "What did you do?"

Flora didn't answer. Her eyes were wide and unblinking.

Like she'd opened a door inside herself and couldn't close it again.

Back in the car, the sat nav refused to locate them.

The signal bars flickered between full and none. Time skipped. At one point, the car clock read 14:26, then jumped to 03:07, then back again. Eve didn't know whether to trust it or smash it.

Mara drove in silence.

They passed signs that hadn't been there before.

Not new ones.

Old ones—weather-worn, half-rotted, with towns that no longer existed. One read *Beaminster – 18 Miles*. Another simply said *The Known Ends Here*.

Eve checked the map on her phone.

No such places. No such road.

"We didn't just shut the loop," she murmured. "We *unhooked* from the map they had us on."

Mara glanced sideways. "What does that mean?"

"It means we're not on the path they planned anymore."

"You say that like it's a good thing."

Eve hesitated.

Then: "It might not be."

They stopped at a petrol station with no name.

A man stood behind the counter, reading a newspaper that looked like it was printed in 1987.

He didn't speak.

Just pointed toward the back room when Flora asked to use the toilet.

Mara grabbed snacks like a reflex.

Eve picked up a bottle of water and froze.

The label.

It didn't have a brand.

Just a sentence printed in a perfect serif font:

"YOU WERE HERE BEFORE."

She put it down carefully.

Flora returned from the back room pale.

"There's no mirror," she whispered. "Just a wall with scribbles."

Eve asked, "What did it say?"

Flora didn't meet her eyes.

"It said: *AVA is not the worst thing they made.*"

Silence folded around them like a fresh bruise.

Mara dropped the snacks.

"We need help. From someone who wasn't part of the experiment. Someone who knew Vivienne before all this."

Eve nodded slowly.

"I know who."

They left the station.

An hour down the coast road, they turned off onto a gravel path lined with trees that looked like they'd been burnt and frozen in the same hour.

At the end: a weathered house.

Isolated.

Vines creeping like veins up the brick.

A postbox with no name—just a scratched-out word and a symbol: ∴

Mara muttered, "What is this place?"

Eve stepped out of the car.

And said quietly, "It's where Vivienne sent everything she couldn't destroy."

Inside the house, it smelled of soil and ink.

A library with no order. Books piled like barricades. Maps pinned to the ceiling. On the far wall, a huge corkboard covered in polaroids, medical scans, tarot cards, children's drawings, and pages torn from technical manuals.

In the centre, as if waiting, stood a woman in her late sixties.

Tall.

Severe.

Hair pulled tight, silver streaks like scars in black wool.

Her voice was not kind. It didn't try to be.

"So," she said, without turning around.

"You finally broke the loop."

Eve swallowed. "You knew?"

The woman turned.

Her eyes were jet black.

And utterly familiar.

"You're not supposed to exist," Eve whispered.

The woman turned fully now, arms crossed, posture precise.

"I'm not the only one."

Her voice was low, refined, with the exacting tone of someone used to finishing other people's sentences. Her black eyes—identical to Ava's—didn't blink often. They measured.

"You can call me **Dr Vale**," she said. "But I imagine you're more interested in what I was before that."

Eve nodded slowly. "You're her. The original."

Flora's breath caught.

Mara blinked. "The original *what*?"

Eve took a step forward, almost reverently.

"The first version. Before Vivienne had a lab. Before she had a theory. Before Ava. Before any of us."

Dr Vale inclined her head. "Prototype Zero."

Mara swore under her breath. "You're telling me she started with you?"

"Not started. *Ended.* I was the edge of her belief system. Everything after me was dilution, distraction or disguise."

Eve's mind reeled. "But you were her sister. Weren't you?"

"She was mine," Vale corrected. "And I loved her. But not in any way you'd understand."

She turned, walked back into the shadows of the room, and gestured for them to follow.

They moved through a study lined with annotated blueprints and handwritten notes.

On the centre table lay a thick folder marked **UNRAVELLING EVENTS – ITERATION L**.

Inside: pages of cross-referenced identities, each bearing combinations of three core initials: E, M, and F.

Mara pointed. "Eve. Mara. Flora."

"And Ava," Eve added. "The inversion."

Vale nodded. "Vivienne didn't care about names. She cared about *symmetries*. About how different combinations of traits could yield different ethical, emotional and psychological outcomes."

Flora's voice was faint. "Outcomes?"

"She didn't see you as people. She saw you as formulations. Ingredients. If one version collapsed under grief, she'd rerun the loop. If one snapped under love, she'd record it. Adjust. Restart."

Mara bristled. "That's monstrous."

Vale looked at her. "So is grief. Vivienne just made it a system."

She moved to a wall chart marked **EMOTIONAL REPLICATION INDEX**.

Dozens of lines intersecting in chaotic precision. Like a metro map of pain.

Eve stared.

One line ran darker than the others. It started with *E* and looped back through *A*, again and again, until it split in two.

"What's this?"

Vale stepped beside her.

"That's *you*. The original Eve strand. The only one that didn't break under remorse."

"And this split?"

"You initiated something that couldn't be replicated. A form of grief that turned to moral clarity instead of collapse."

Flora's hands trembled. "That's why they needed Ava."

"Exactly. Ava was designed to carry the excess. But somewhere along the way... she became an echo with its own voice."

Mara glanced at the scattered charts.

"So what now? You help us shut this down?"

Vale shook her head.

"You already did. That's why things are *wrong* out there."

She pointed toward the cracked sky through the window.

"You've untethered the feedback loop. The world they built on top of your pain is now *unmapped*. That makes it *dangerous*."

Eve looked at her. "For who?"

Vale's voice dropped.

"For everyone who was stitched into it."

Flora spoke suddenly.

"They'll come for us."

"They already are," Vale said, turning to a second screen now coming to life. "This place is still off-grid, but it won't hold. The signal you broke sent ripples through every failed outcome."

She pulled up a screen showing security footage from locations labelled *Iteration B – Failed Merge* and *Loop K – Corrupted*.

The images were glitching.

People walking backwards.

Rain falling upward.

Children standing still while time moved around them.

Eve whispered, "They're unravelling."

Vale nodded.

"And they'll reach for whatever they can to re-stabilise. Which means *you*."

Mara reached for the table. "Then let them come."

But Eve didn't move.

She was staring at a single still frame on the monitor.

A person watching them.

From behind the petrol station counter.

Unblinking.

Wearing a coat stitched with the word **GENTIAN**.

Eve's lips parted.

"That's not a person."

Vale's voice was barely a whisper.

"No. That's a *collector*."

The image on the monitor didn't move.

The figure—tall, sexless, standing too straight—was fixed at the edge of the petrol station counter, half-shaded by a stack of paper towels. But the longer Eve stared, the more she realised something was *wrong* with the stillness. It wasn't absence of movement. It was **perfect symmetry**. Every joint too aligned. Every shadow too *unbroken*.

Mara leaned closer. "Who the hell is Gentian?"

Vale didn't answer immediately. She flicked the monitor off instead.

Then said: "They're not a *who*. They're a retrieval protocol."

Eve turned slowly. "Like a bounty hunter?"

"No. Like a correctional virus."

Flora moved to the window. Her breath fogged the glass.

"The woman in the coat... she spoke to me. Once. Years ago. In the woods behind the foster home."

Vale looked up. "Did she ask you to choose something?"

Flora nodded. "A card. She said I had to choose one and burn the others."

Eve's chest tightened. "What card?"

Flora shook her head. "I can't remember. Just that it had my own handwriting on it. And it wasn't something I'd written yet."

Mara stepped back. "This is getting insane."

Vale didn't blink.

"You think it's insane *now*?"

She moved to a drawer and pulled out a small metal case.

Inside: five paper cards, each faded and uneven. Each with a name in different handwriting:

- **Eve**

- **Mara**

- **Flora**

- **Ava**

- **V—** *(the final letter scratched out)*

"These were loop tokens," Vale said. "Each time a subject began to fragment, a token would be delivered—physically or metaphysically. To anchor the identity. Or to warn of its degradation."

Flora whispered, "But who delivered them?"

Vale looked at the darkened monitor.

"Gentian. They're not human. Not machine. Just... an interface for unfinished grief."

Eve's throat tightened.

"They're coming, aren't they?"

"They're already inside," Vale murmured.

Mara swore and backed toward the door. "We need to move. Now."

Vale stopped her. "If you leave through the wrong door, you'll just loop again. This house has *re-entry triggers*. That's how I've stayed here undetected."

Flora pointed at a narrow hallway. "What about that one?"

"No," Vale snapped. "That leads to the failed Ava split. It's flooded with recursion."

Mara, fed up, spun around and said, "Then what do we do?"

Vale finally relented.

"You split."

Eve frowned. "Split what?"

"Yourselves. Two go forward. One goes sideways. It's the only way to confuse the collectors. They can't trace fragmented emotional threads easily. Especially not yours."

Silence fell.

No one moved.

Then Flora stepped forward.

"I'll go sideways."

Eve grabbed her wrist. "You don't have to."

"I do," she said simply. "I remember something else now. From the woods. After the card. She whispered in my ear—*The side route saves the others. But it will cost your face.*"

Mara blinked. "What does that mean?"

Vale didn't answer.

Just whispered, "It means she'll forget who she is. For a while."

Flora smiled. "That's happened before."

They moved quickly.

Vale activated an old switch hidden beneath the hearth rug.

A trapdoor slid open—revealing two diverging tunnels: one clean, white-lit, medical in aesthetic; the other narrow and earthy, with roots breaking through the walls like veins through skin.

Vale handed each of them a vial of liquid.

"Memory stabilisers," she said. "They'll keep your core identity intact for seventy-two hours."

Mara tucked hers into her boot.

Flora didn't pocket hers.

She drank it there and then.

And smiled, softly. "Just in case."

They hugged tightly.

Flora went first—into the earthy tunnel, barefoot.

Eve turned to Vale. "Where does hers lead?"

Vale replied, "To a place where memories speak first. And faces follow."

Mara nodded grimly. "And ours?"

Vale turned to the clean tunnel. "To where the programme began. The source. The last operational facility Vivienne ever touched."

She looked them dead in the eye.

"You'll either end this. Or be rewritten."

The tunnel doors closed behind them.

And for the first time, **the loop didn't restart**.

It fractured.

The tunnel hummed as they walked.

Clean. Fluorescent. Smooth underfoot like glass that had forgotten it was once sand. Mara walked ahead, gun drawn but hands steady, her breath slow and contained. Eve followed in silence, fingers grazing the cool metal wall, as if trying to pick up a vibration only she could hear.

They didn't speak until the corridor opened into a hexagonal chamber.

In the centre: a stairwell descending into a pit of light.

No signs.

No buttons.

Just a panel marked:
REPLICATION ARCHIVE: INITIATE KEY = [V]

Eve exhaled. "It's her."

Mara looked at the stairs. "You're sure?"

"No. But my *bones* are."

They descended.

The air shifted.

Not in temperature—but in pressure. The deeper they went, the heavier it felt to think. Like their thoughts were being intercepted mid-formation and catalogued somewhere else.

When they reached the bottom, the light dimmed.

A door slid open without a sound.

And inside the chamber sat a single figure.

Wearing a black shift dress.

Face obscured by a mesh veil.

Fingertips resting on the arms of a padded chair as if she'd never moved.

Mara lifted her weapon instinctively. "Identify yourself."

The figure didn't flinch.

She simply said, "My name is **Vivienne Vale**."

Eve staggered. "You're *dead*."

The woman smiled. "No. I'm *stored*."

Mara kept the gun raised. "What does that mean?"

The voice—precise, warm, unnerving—continued.

"I exist as an algorithmic echo. A personality map extrapolated from the final Vivienne's cognitive residue. What you see is a shell. What you're speaking to is *her intention*."

Eve stepped forward.

"Why are you still running?"

Vivienne-Vale's head tilted. "Because not all grief can be buried. Some of it loops until it becomes the system."

Eve's breath caught.

"She didn't just build the experiments. She *fed* them. With herself."

Vivienne-Vale nodded.

"She found the edge of her loss. Then replicated it. Again and again. Until it became *architecture*."

Mara lowered the gun slightly. "This whole thing... it wasn't just about pain tolerance, was it?"

"No," said the voice. "It was about **preservation**. A sanctuary for unresolved suffering. The idea was simple: if you could loop your grief, contain it, rehearse it, perhaps one day... it would resolve itself."

Eve whispered, "Did it?"

Vivienne-Vale's tone flattened. "No. It began to mutate. The loops stopped mimicking grief and started manufacturing identity."

Screens lit up along the chamber walls.

Footage. Files. Moments they remembered—and moments they *didn't*. Alternate realities, echo decisions, versions of themselves with different scars. One showed Eve and Ava *hugging*. Another showed Mara *dying*. A third showed Flora with her eyes gouged out, smiling calmly.

Mara looked away.

"This is obscene."

"It is *complete*," said the voice. "You are not survivors. You are iterations. Your loop wasn't the first successful one—it was the first one to end *without instruction*."

Eve backed against the wall. "Then why bring us here?"

Vivienne-Vale answered gently.

"Because you've reached the loop's natural conclusion. There is only one final act left."

A console slid out of the floor.

On it: a small device, like a fingerprint reader fused with a key.

Vivienne-Vale said: "One of you must press. It will execute either **termination** or **total migration**."

Mara frowned. "Migration?"

"Everything—the data, the loop code, the echoes—migrated into one surviving identity."

Eve's voice cracked. "And termination?"

"The loop is deleted. And all copies with it."

Mara stepped toward the device.

Then stopped.

"So we pick between carrying it... or killing it."

Eve whispered, "No. Between *becoming her*. Or letting her die."

Suddenly, a high-pitched sound rang out.

Not from the chamber.

From *inside Eve's chest*.

The vial in her pocket—the stabiliser Vale had given her—was glowing.

And pulsing.

Vivienne-Vale's voice dipped into something almost affectionate.

"Ah. You're the carrier. Of course."

Mara turned. "What the hell does that mean?"

"It means the loop code has already chosen her."

Eve looked down at her trembling hands.

"She *is* the final container."

The light from the vial grew brighter.

Mara reached for her.

But the chamber pulsed.

And the door behind them locked shut.

The vial in Eve's pocket vibrated like a trapped heartbeat.

Not fast. Just relentless.

She took it out slowly. The glow was no longer white, but a shifting amber. Like firelight inside glass.

Mara stared at it. "What happens if it breaks?"

Vivienne-Vale answered without emotion. "Then the loop collapses inward. Recursive implosion. Every strand of identity caught inside will be nullified."

"Meaning—?"

"Meaning none of you will ever have existed."

Eve closed her fingers around the vial.

It felt hot. Not physically. *Spiritually*. Like it recognised her.

Like it had been *waiting*.

Vivienne-Vale's voice softened. "There is a kind of mercy in erasure, Eve. To choose silence over endless simulation."

Mara turned on her. "You don't get to moralise. You're a *ghost in a folder*."

"I am Vivienne's last intention," the echo replied. "You, Mara, are nothing but a deviation."

Mara stepped toward her.

"Say that again."

Vivienne's voice sharpened. "You weren't supposed to survive. Your loop was cut. You re-entered by *bleeding through*. A corruption."

Eve snapped. "Stop."

Silence fell.

And then—

The console lit up.

Two options:

1. MIGRATION – Fuse All Surviving Consciousnesses into Primary Host

2. TERMINATION – Cleanse Loop and Null All Residual Echoes

A single glowing square awaited Eve's fingerprint.

Mara whispered, "Don't touch it yet. Just breathe."

But Eve was already seeing things she shouldn't.

Visions bleeding through the walls of her mind.

Ava laughing beside her in the forest, their hands sticky with cherry juice.

Flora braiding her hair at a sleepover that never happened.

Vivienne's voice in a dream, whispering, *You are the house I built to mourn myself in.*

Eve closed her eyes.

And raised her hand.

Then—

A crack of static.
A *third* square appeared on the console.

3. OVERRIDE – Proxy Intervention Detected

The chamber lights flickered.

Vivienne-Vale froze.

Her voice crackled. "This is not authorised—"

But the screen now displayed a new name:

FLORA VALE (ALT STRAND 6C)

Mara stepped back. "She's alive. She's *inside*."

A low hum filled the air—then a voice that wasn't quite Flora's, and not quite digital.

"I remembered the card. It said: 'The loop breaks with love.'"

Eve dropped the vial.

It didn't shatter.

It *melted*, dissolving into vapour.

The console screamed, flickering between commands.

Then the chamber split.

Literally.

The walls cracked apart, splitting the space into six floating segments.

Mara grabbed Eve's wrist.

"We need to go. Now."

Vivienne-Vale's voice became distorted, panicked.

"You'll kill everything. You'll kill *her*—"

But the screens now showed something else.

Gentian.

Crumbling.

Not walking. Not chasing.

Folding.

As if the world had lost the will to remember it.

Eve ran.

Mara beside her.

The ground beneath them became less solid, like time itself was thinning.

Eve looked up.

Through the cracked ceiling, through the fading sky.

She saw Flora.

Standing in a forest that didn't exist anymore.

Smiling.

Holding the same card from years ago.

Only now it read:
"You chose the others."

The system was collapsing.

Not explosively—but like the end of a long-held breath. Quiet. Reluctant. As if the world itself was admitting it had gone on too long.

Eve and Mara burst through a flickering threshold of light, the last remnants of the facility warping behind them. Floors peeled away. Walls receded like retreating tidewater. And overhead, a thunderless sky emptied of colour.

Time did not slow. It simply forgot.

They emerged into an orchard that didn't belong to either of them.

Apples overripe on branches that bowed too low.

A river nearby shimmered without movement.

Mara caught her breath. "Are we out?"

Eve nodded—but cautiously. "We're *somewhere else*."

They turned.

No door. No frame. No tunnel.

Only the orchard, and beyond it, a crooked house with no windows—just mirrors nailed where glass should have been.

Mara exhaled. "That's not creepy at all."

Eve didn't speak.

Because her reflection wasn't hers.

In the mirror: Ava.

Younger. Hair unbrushed. Eyes clear.

She mouthed something.

Not "help." Not "run."

But **"Remember."**

Eve stepped closer.

The image didn't follow her movement. It stayed still. As if pre-recorded.

She placed a hand to the glass.

The image rippled.

And then vanished.

Mara whispered, "This isn't over."

"No," Eve replied. "It's just *different* now."

A breeze passed through the orchard, though no trees moved.

And then came the click.

Sharp. Mechanical.

A small device had landed at their feet.

Smooth, black. The size of a pocket watch.

On its surface: a symbol—interlocking rings shaped like an infinity loop twisted into a question mark.

Eve bent to pick it up.

The moment her fingers touched it, a message played:

> "This is Gentian fallback protocol. Iteration complete. Host deviation accepted. Residual data transferred to Unit C."

Eve looked up.

Mara frowned. "What's Unit C?"

A voice behind them answered.

"*Me.*"

They turned.

A young girl—eight, maybe nine—stood in the grass barefoot.

Wearing a long coat several sizes too big.

Hair like straw. Skin like milk.

Eyes like Vivienne.

But she wasn't *her*.

Not quite.

Eve's voice trembled. "Who are you?"

The girl tilted her head, owl-like.

"I'm what's left when grief is removed from identity."

Mara's hand twitched near her hip. "And what does that mean, exactly?"

The girl smiled.

"It means I'm *clean*."

Silence stretched.

Then the girl sat on the ground and began building a small pile of stones.

Nothing menacing.

Just… deliberate.

Eve moved toward her, slowly.

"If you're the residue... why are you here?"

The girl didn't look up.

"Because the system still needs a shape. And you're not going to give it one."

Eve crouched beside her.

"Then who will?"

The girl placed the final stone.

Then looked directly at her.

"You left space. So now I will fill it."

Mara stepped forward. "Is that a threat?"

"No. It's balance."

Eve whispered, "Are you... going to hurt us?"

The girl smiled sweetly. Innocently.

Like every child who's ever drawn a monster and said it was a friend.

"Not unless you try to fix me."

The air changed again.

The orchard dimmed.

The girl stood, turned, and walked toward the house of mirrored windows.

Each reflection now showing **someone different**.

Ava.

Vivienne.

Flora.

Even Mara.

But not Eve.

Not anymore.

Eve turned to Mara. "Did we win?"

Mara hesitated.

Then: "We broke the loop. But something else got through."

They stood there in the stillness, two shadows beneath a sky still deciding what season to be.

Somewhere behind them, a new system was already starting to hum.

Chapter 7

They woke to birdsong that sounded *too perfect*.

Not quite real—like a recording of nature playing on loop.

Eve sat up slowly, a blanket of mist hovering just above the grass. The orchard had changed again. The trees were now in bloom, heavy with blossom, no sign of the apples from before. Petals fell, suspended mid-air, never quite reaching the ground. As if even gravity was taking its time deciding.

Mara stirred beside her, squinting at the horizon. "This place…"

"It's not real," Eve finished. "Or it's *not finished*."

They both turned toward the crooked house.

And saw the girl—Unit C—standing barefoot on the roof, arms outstretched, eyes closed, **absorbing the morning like a prayer**.

"She's… building," Eve whispered.

Mara nodded. "Or *rewriting*."

The house had grown. There were now chimneys where none had been. Ivy that hadn't existed hours earlier. The ground around it had shifted shape too—a garden appeared, its soil neatly furrowed, though no one had touched it.

"She's designing memory," Mara muttered.

"Not just memory," Eve said. "Meaning."

Unit C opened her eyes and looked directly at them.

Then spoke—without moving her mouth.

"Will you help me shape the story?"

They followed her voice across the field.

By the time they reached the house, it had changed again.

No mirrors now—just stained-glass windows. But not of saints or angels. These windows bore *portraits*—figures they recognised only slightly. Past versions of themselves, caught mid-expression, as though lifted from moments they'd forgotten.

Flora laughing in a classroom.

Mara bleeding from a wound that didn't exist.

Ava asleep in a bath.

And at the centre, one final frame.

Empty.

Waiting.

Inside the house, Unit C stood in a room with no ceiling, under an open sky.

In the centre: a low table, with a thick book resting on top.

She looked at Eve. "This is the new loop. But it doesn't repeat. It evolves."

Mara frowned. "You said you were clean."

"I am," she replied. "But I still require *narrative*. Otherwise, the grief leaks back in."

Eve approached the book.

It was blank—except the first line:

> *Once upon a silence, a woman chose not to fix what broke her.*

Mara leaned in. "Is this about us?"

The girl smiled. "It's not about anything. Yet. But if you stay, you'll be written into it."

"And if we leave?" Eve asked.

"You'll forget," the girl said simply. "Not everything. Just enough to survive."

Eve glanced at Mara.

Mara didn't speak.

They both knew the weight of what they were being offered:

To become part of something… again.
To be folded into a story that may never end, but might at least *make sense*.

Or to walk away with incomplete memory, carrying only fragments of what happened.

Neither option was mercy.

Both were beginnings.

Suddenly, the book flipped pages on its own.

Then stopped.

A new sentence appeared:

> *She chose to write the ending herself.*

Unit C looked up, eyes burning with quiet fire.

"That wasn't me."

Mara whispered, "Then who?"

Footsteps echoed behind them.

They turned—

And saw **Flora**.

But older.

Changed.

Wearing clothes from *another life*.

And in her hand, a pen that glowed.

Flora didn't smile.

She didn't need to.

Her presence alone felt like punctuation—something that came **after** everything else.

She stood in the threshold of the mirrorless house, her silhouette outlined by a light that came from nowhere. Older now. Not aged, but *refined*. Sharper. As if each year had been cut out of someone else and worn with deliberate weight.

The glowing pen in her hand pulsed like a heartbeat.

Eve's mouth went dry. "How are you alive?"

"I'm not," Flora replied. "Not in the way you mean."

She stepped into the house, bare feet on polished wooden floors that hadn't existed seconds ago.

"The override wasn't just a failsafe. It was a seed. Vivienne designed every loop to fail eventually—because it was her grief pretending to be closure. But I made a different kind of loop. One that evolves. One that knows how to *end*."

Unit C tilted her head. "But you left space. You abandoned function."

"I left *choice*," Flora replied. "There's a difference."

Mara stepped forward, arms crossed. "So what are you now? The architect? The author?"

Flora looked at her evenly.

"I'm the part of Vivienne that *stopped blaming everyone else*."

The book on the table began to flicker.

Its surface glitching.

Sentences appearing and vanishing in bursts.

One said:

> *Grief is not sacred. It's just heavy.*

Another:

> *Pain is clever. It'll become anyone you feed it to.*

Eve sat down in the chair opposite the book.

"This story... it's not a loop anymore. It's a weapon."

Flora nodded. "Yes. But only if you let it write *you*. That's what Vivienne never understood—control doesn't mean *stability*. It means stagnation. And stagnation festers."

Mara exhaled sharply. "You want us to what—co-author this thing with you?"

"I want you to decide," Flora said. "Write with me. Or wipe it clean."

Unit C frowned. "That's not protocol."

"No," Flora said. "It's rebellion."

She laid the pen on the book.

The light dimmed.

And for a moment, there was only the sound of wind moving through a forest that didn't exist.

Eve looked at the pen.

Then at the girl.

Then at Flora.

And then she said, "Before we do anything... I want to *see* what Vivienne left behind. I want to see all of it."

Flora nodded once. "You're sure?"

"I need to know the shape of her grief before I decide if it's worth keeping."

Unit C looked up sharply.

"Then I'll show you."

The room dissolved.

Not exploded—just fell away.

Wood became memory. Air became static.

And then they were standing on a shoreline made of salt.

The ocean ahead shimmered, but it didn't move.

Behind them, instead of the house, a *theatre* stood.

Broken. Half-burned.

A sign above it read:

**THE LIFE OF VIVIENNE
ONE NIGHT ONLY
(NO REFUNDS. NO RE-ENTRY.)**

Mara rolled her eyes. "Subtle."

Flora smiled faintly. "She was always dramatic."

They walked inside.

No audience.

Just a stage lit by a single spotlight.

On it: a younger Vivienne Vale.

Not speaking. Just crying.

Over and over again.

Each sob looping.
Each gasp identical.
An endless cycle of expression without relief.

Eve stepped closer.

And saw that her *tears were made of mirrors.*

Every time one fell, it reflected someone else's face.

Flora said softly, "This was the root. Vivienne didn't want to be remembered. She wanted to be *witnessed*. That's why her pain grew faces."

Mara shook her head. "So she turned us into characters."

Flora whispered, "Yes. But we don't have to stay written."

Behind the curtain, another scene began to unfold.

Vivienne teaching a child to lie.

Vivienne staging her own breakdown for sympathy.

Vivienne copying the voice of a therapist and pretending it was her own.

The system hadn't protected her grief.

It had curated it.

Eve reached for the pen again.

And this time, the book opened to a blank page that smelled faintly of salt.

"Let's write something else," she said.

Unit C blinked. "What if it becomes worse?"

Flora answered without hesitation.

"Then we *start again*. That's what she was too afraid to do."

The pen vibrated in Eve's hand like it didn't want to be held.

She glanced at the page. The blank space no longer looked passive. It *waited*. Like something with breath. With preference.

Eve wrote the first line.

> *There was a day when the loop blinked first.*

The pen glowed.

The room did not respond immediately—but the air got heavier.

Unit C took a step back, her mouth slightly parted. Not in fear.

In recognition.

"You've changed the tone," she whispered. "The system doesn't like tone shifts."

Flora smirked. "Good."

Eve kept writing.

> *She didn't erase what hurt her. She studied it until it stopped lying.*

The light overhead dimmed.

The theatre shuddered.

Cracks ran through the floor like veins.

Mara said, "We need to get out of this memory. It's not just reacting—it's trying to rewrite *us* now."

Flora nodded. "It'll come for your roots. Whatever parts of you still need her to make sense."

Eve paused.

Her next line appeared slowly:

> *What if I don't need sense anymore? What if I need space?*

That was the tipping point.

The theatre combusted—not into flame, but into *expression*.

Every wall, every surface, exploded outward in symbols.

The exit sign dissolved into a hundred red butterflies.

The stage lights turned into twin moons and hung overhead like waiting eyes.

Vivienne's looping sob became birdsong—then static—then silence.

Mara grabbed Eve's arm. "Write *faster!*"

But Eve wasn't scared.

The more she wrote, the more *herself* she felt.

It wasn't narrative. It was *agency*.

A rebellion written in cursive.

Behind them, a wall cracked open.

A passage appeared—narrow and made of stitched-together film reels.

Flora said, "That's the spine. The oldest part of the construct."

Unit C looked unsure. "It won't like you going there."

Mara cracked her knuckles. "It doesn't *like* anything."

They stepped through.

Instant darkness.

The reels beneath their feet flickered under pressure. Scenes burst underfoot—memories, deleted lines, half-spoken regrets.

Vivienne's voice echoed faintly:

"Don't take it from me. It's the only thing that ever held."

Eve whispered, "She meant the system. The grief. The loop."

Flora added, "She clung to it like love."

At the end of the corridor, a vault.

Covered in etched names—every variant and version of every person the system had ever simulated.

Some were familiar.

Most weren't.

Mara placed her hand on the door.

It hissed.

Unsealed.

Inside: a single chair, floating in a room of black static.

And on that chair:

A woman with no face.

Not metaphorical.

Literally blank. Smooth.

But as Eve stepped closer, the woman turned slightly—and her body posture, her breathing, the way her hands folded—

It was Vivienne.

Or *what was left* of her.

Flora whispered, "The mother fragment."

Unit C nodded. "That's what drives everything. Not code. *Her longing.*"

The pen in Eve's hand glowed again—hot this time.

The book reappeared, hovering mid-air.

A line wrote itself:

> *This is where grief becomes programming. Decide if it still deserves your data.*

Eve hesitated.

Mara stepped beside her.

"You're not here to fix her. You're here to *end* her."

Eve looked at the woman in the chair.

At the absence of a face.

And she said softly, "No. I'm here to *unplug* her."

She raised the pen.

And drew a single line through the air.

A cut.

The static went still.

Then—

The woman exhaled.

Collapsed inward.

No sound. No collapse.

Just... deletion.

The vault dissolved into mist.

The corridor behind them blinked out.

And all that remained was the echo of a new phrase:

> *You can't grieve forever. Eventually, the dead stop asking to be remembered.*

They stood in the silence.

Flora wiped her eyes. "That was the real override."

Unit C sat cross-legged on the floor, pressing her palm to the static.

"Then what am I now?"

Eve crouched beside her.

"You're what comes *after* grief. Possibility."

And as the room faded—

A garden began to grow where the vault once stood.

No design.

No intention.

Just roots.

Finally free.

The world returned as mist first.

Then outlines.

Then weight.

Eve blinked and found herself standing in a quiet field that shimmered faintly, as if light couldn't decide which direction to fall in. There were no buildings. No markers. Just a single path carved gently into the grass, leading somewhere she didn't recognise.

Behind her, the vault was gone. The theatre, the orchard, the mirrors. All of it—dismantled like a stage set after the final performance.

Unit C stood beside her.

But something had changed.

She was taller now. Older, even. The innocence had dimmed, replaced by something that resembled *choice*.

"I kept what I needed," she said, without prompting.

"What did you let go of?" Eve asked.

The girl tilted her head. "The need to be believed."

Further down the path, Mara emerged—clothes dusty, hair windblown, eyes bloodshot but awake.

"I had a memory," she said, breathless. "I think it was real."

Eve waited.

Mara continued. "I saw myself before the loop. Years ago. Before I ever met Vivienne. I was in a bus station, writing a postcard to no one."

"What did it say?"

"*Don't find me. I'm still deciding who I want to be.*"

Eve touched her arm. "Then maybe that's what this is. The space where we decide again."

They walked together now, the three of them.

No need for destination. Just movement.

And as they walked, the world around them began to take form. But not as it was before.

This wasn't restoration.

It was *creation*.

A language of soil and sky and unspoken futures.

A deer watched them from the treeline.

A wind passed by that smelled faintly of ozone and rosemary.

No clocks. No systems. Just sensation.

And then they heard the bell.

Once.

Twice.

Three times.

Up ahead, a building emerged.

Not Vivienne's facility.

Not the orchard house.

Something… simpler.

A schoolhouse, maybe. Painted white, with green shutters and a door slightly ajar. Smoke curling from its chimney.

Eve paused. "This place wasn't in the construct."

"No," Unit C said. "It's been waiting outside it."

They entered.

Inside, the air was warm. Wooden floors, worn with history. A single desk, on which sat a note.

Mara picked it up.

Welcome back. We've saved your place.
You don't have to perform anymore.

Flora stood in the corner.

Her voice low. "I found this before I found you."

She walked to the desk and opened the drawer.

Inside: a mirror.

But this time, it didn't reflect the past.

It reflected the *possibility of a self unobserved*.

No narrative. No damage. No plot.

Just *being*.

Flora looked at Eve. "The final test isn't escape. It's existence without explanation."

Mara let out a low laugh. "That's harder than any loop."

Unit C stepped forward. "So what now?"

Eve smiled.

It wasn't joyful. It wasn't resolved.

But it was *real*.

"Now we live without being written."

In the days that followed—though no one counted them—they made a garden.

Not symbolic.

Just vegetables.

And sometimes wildflowers.

Unit C changed her name.

Flora kept her coat.

Mara learned to sleep without waking in panic.

And Eve?

She planted rosemary.

Because it didn't ask to be remembered.

It just grew.

It began with a rustling.

Not wind.

Not animals.

Something *beneath*.

Eve was tending the garden—knees deep in soil, hands stained with the kind of quiet satisfaction she hadn't known in years—when she felt the tremor.

Small.

Rhythmic.

Like breath beneath a blanket.

She froze. Listened. And then reached into the earth.

Her fingers met something soft. Not organic. Not plant. Fabric?

No.

It was parchment.

She pulled it out slowly.

A folded letter, brittle but warm.

Unmarked. No address. No signature.

But the paper hummed with familiarity. Like touching a childhood photograph you don't remember taking but *feel* in your chest.

Eve opened it.

The handwriting was neat. Measured. Vivienne's.

I couldn't kill the seed. So I left it somewhere only you would find it.
If it grows, you'll know it wasn't grief.
It was love.
And love... rewrites everything.

She read the letter twice.

Then again.

Then she stood, silent, the garden around her suddenly too quiet.

Mara was inside, polishing a kettle.

Flora was asleep, curled in the window seat, a book open on her chest.

Unit C—now calling herself "Neve"—was barefoot in the field, turning slowly in circles, eyes closed, smiling at the sun.

Eve tucked the letter into her pocket and walked toward the edge of the vegetable beds.

There, where she'd planted the rosemary, something *else* had begun to sprout.

Not herbs.

Not weeds.

Paper.

Thin, pale stalks pushing up from the earth—sheets unfurling like petals. Each one covered in *Vivienne's handwriting*.

She crouched and touched one.

It didn't vanish.

Didn't disintegrate.

It purred under her fingertips.

Alive.

Neve approached quietly, her voice gentle. "Something wrong?"

Eve shook her head. "I don't think so. But I don't think it's… finished."

They watched as one of the pages split and revealed something inside—like a seed cracking open.

A *tiny, mechanical bird* emerged.

Wings trembling.

It looked at them.

Tilted its head.

And spoke.

In Vivienne's voice.

"If you're hearing this, it means I got better at grief."

Mara appeared behind them, coffee mug in hand. "Please tell me that's not another loop starting."

The bird turned toward her.

"It's not a loop. It's a gift. You can ignore it. You can bury it. Or—"

It paused.

"You can teach it to fly."

Then it leapt into the air—erratic, wobbling, confused.

But flying.

Sort of.

It landed clumsily on the fence and chirped.

A sound that *didn't echo*.

Didn't repeat.

Just existed.

Once.

Neve looked at Eve. "Is it safe?"

"I don't know."

Flora stepped outside, yawning. "What are we all looking at?"

Mara raised her mug. "Grief. Evolved."

The bird blinked.

Then dissolved into mist.

Not like deletion.

More like... choice.

Eve looked down at the rosemary.

It still stood.

Unbothered.

Unmoved.

But growing.

Always growing.

She reached into the soil once more—just to feel it.

Just to *touch* what remains.

And found...

Nothing.

Just earth.

Just now.

Eve sat alone in the evening light, a piece of paper on her lap, the pen warm between her fingers.

The others were inside now—voices drifting faintly through the wooden walls, laughter woven between spoon clinks and floor creaks. It wasn't loud. It wasn't dramatic. But it was life, and for the first time in longer than she could remember, she wasn't trying to *contain* it.

The bird was gone.

The garden was still.

And the soil felt honest.

So she began to write.

Not to Vivienne.

Not to the system.

But to herself.

Dear girl who tried so hard,

I see you now.

You weren't weak for surviving her. You were *clever* for slipping out of her story without screaming.

You let grief believe it had you. You let shame take the stage. But even when the mirror told you your name in someone else's voice—you kept *breathing*.

That was the beginning.

She paused.

The light shifted on the page.

She continued.

You were never broken. You were badly *narrated*.

That's all.

Vivienne told the story. But you felt it. And feeling is the only thing that doesn't need proof.

I'm proud of you.

I'm sorry I tried to forget you.

I won't do that again.

She signed it simply:

E.

Folded the paper.

And stood.

At the edge of the rosemary bed, she dug a small hole with her hands.

Not deep.

Just enough to *place* something.

She laid the letter in the soil, pressed it down softly, then covered it.

Nothing symbolic.

No ceremony.

Just closure.

And as she stood to leave, she didn't feel release.

She felt *return*.

To herself.

To the unwritten version.

To the truth beyond repetition.

Inside, the table was set for four.

Flora was telling a story that made Neve roll her eyes and Mara grin without restraint.

The kettle boiled.

The window fogged.

And when Eve stepped back inside, nobody asked where she'd been.

They made space.

A plate appeared.

A mug.

A laugh.

And something quiet passed between them all:

Not memory.

Not meaning.

Just *presence*.

She sat down.

Picked up her fork.

And the story, finally, stopped needing to be told.

Chapter 8

It started with the door.

Not a knock.

Not even a sound.

Just... a presence.

Eve had grown used to the hush of this new life—the scratch of Neve's pen on the windowsill each morning, the kettle's low whistle, the garden breathing beneath her fingertips. The air had memory, but no demands. The days didn't declare themselves. They *unfolded*.

But that morning, as she passed the old white door to fetch rosemary for breakfast, she *knew*.

Someone—or something—was on the other side.

Waiting.

She didn't touch the handle.

She didn't need to.

It pulsed.

Faintly.

As if sensing her proximity. The wood was warm. Not from the sun. From *attention*.

Mara stepped out from the pantry, holding a chipped bowl. "You feel it too?"

Eve nodded. "How long has it been like this?"

"Since before I woke up," she said quietly. "I didn't want to say anything. I thought maybe it was just me."

Neve appeared behind them. Her face was flushed from running—she'd been playing with shadows again, chasing the wind through the tall grass like it owed her something.

But now, she was still.

"That door's not *ours* anymore," she whispered.

Flora was last to speak.

She leaned against the far wall, arms crossed, eyes narrowed. She looked older again. More herself. Whatever that now meant.

"We broke the loop," she said. "So anything that's still trying to find us... doesn't belong."

Eve placed her hand on the handle.

The pulse deepened.

Not aggressive.

Just *present*.

Like a song you hadn't heard in years, but recognised instantly.

"It knows me," she said softly.

They waited.

But the door didn't open.

It didn't force its way in.

It *offered*.

And that was worse.

Vivienne never offered. The system never *invited*. It had always pushed. Overwritten. Claimed.

But this felt... human.

Or close to it.

Neve moved beside Eve, placing a hand on her back. "We don't have to open it."

"I know."

"We could burn it."

"I know."

Mara exhaled. "We could just keep living. Pretend it's not there."

Eve looked at them all.

"I think this is the final test. Not survival. Not resistance. *Permission*."

Flora flinched at that word.

They stepped back and sat around the table in silence.

Let the day pass.

Let the light shift.

No one opened the door.

But it didn't go away.

That evening, the air tasted different.

The garden didn't grow.

The rosemary curled at the edges.

Neve's shadows stopped playing.

And when they lit the fire, the wood refused to catch.

Like the world had gone... hesitant.

Uncertain.

Waiting for something to be acknowledged.

That night, Eve dreamed of a hallway she'd never seen.

Long. Grey. Fluorescent-lit.

And at the end of it—Vivienne.

Not the vivisected memory. Not the system's corrupted mother-core.

Vivienne as she once was.

Hair falling out of its tie. A jumper far too big. Pale blue eyes, but no cruelty in them—just exhaustion. Just *regret*.

She looked up at Eve.

And spoke one line:

"Tell me what you made instead."

Eve woke before dawn.

Her hands already reaching for the pen.

She found the old notebook on the windowsill. The one that used to record loops, code fragments, symptoms.

She turned to a blank page.

And she wrote:

We made meals.
We made silence without ache.
We planted things that didn't ask to be named.
We made a girl who stopped needing to be believed.
We made mornings that didn't apologise for themselves.
We made *each other*.

She paused.

Then added:

And it was enough.

The door was still pulsing.

But now… slower.

Less urgent.

As if it had read the page and decided to wait.

Not demand.

Wait.

Eve closed the notebook.

Looked out the window.

And wondered how long peace could last when the past learns how to knock gently.

It wasn't a vote.

Not officially.

But as the day grew older, the question hovered above them like a high note with no resolve.

What do we do about the door?

It pulsed—always in the background. Not louder, not softer. Just *there*. A heartbeat from another life.

Mara paced.

Flora sharpened a knife that didn't need sharpening.

Neve, usually the first to name fear, refused to speak at all. She sat by the window with a stick of charcoal, drawing circles on the table—loops within loops, none of them closed.

Eve broke the silence.

"We can't keep ignoring it."

That was all it took.

Mara flared.

"Why not? It hasn't done anything. It's not *asking* anything."

Flora snorted. "You think silence means safety?"

Neve finally looked up. "It's *inviting* something. That's worse than an attack."

Eve watched them all.

This was the test, wasn't it?

Not the knock.

The *rift* it caused.

Mara stepped forward, gripping the edge of the counter. "We've earned peace. We broke the loop. We buried Vivienne. We made a garden, Eve. We've *grown*. Why would we even *consider* opening that?"

Flora didn't flinch. "Because peace built on fear is just another kind of prison."

Neve exhaled. "And prisons are where we began."

Eve closed her eyes.

"Then what do you want to do?"

Flora: "Open it. See what remains. End it properly."

Mara: "Ignore it. Starve it. If it needs acknowledgement, let it *rot* in silence."

Neve: "Burn it. If we can't know what it is, destroy it before it learns how to shape itself."

Eve opened her eyes.

Three paths.

Three wounds disguised as choices.

That night, the garden didn't just wilt.

It bled.

Tiny drops of black sap leaked from the bean stalks. The rosemary turned to ash at the root. A rusted nail surfaced from the tomato bed. Not one they'd dropped.

An old one.

From *before*.

Mara screamed when she saw it. Not because of the nail.

Because it had her name engraved in its side.

**M. Cadell
Observation Phase 3.**

They gathered around the firepit, but no one lit it.

There was nothing left to burn.

Neve crouched, holding the nail in her palm. "They catalogued us."

"They did worse than that," Mara muttered. "They *numbered* us."

Flora stayed still. "Then this isn't just a door. It's a sender."

Eve asked, "You think it's transmitting?"

"No," Flora said. "I think it's receiving. Our hesitation. Our tension. Our fear."

Neve's voice cracked. "Then we've fed it too well."

Later, while the others slept, Eve stood by the door again.

This time she brought a piece of charcoal from the table. She pressed it gently to the wood.

It didn't flinch.

She drew a line.

Then another.

Until she had a crude eye etched into the centre of the door.

Not as a threat.

As a *mirror*.

"If you're watching," she whispered, "watch this instead."

She turned her back and walked away.

The pulse faltered.

For the first time.

The silence became less certain.

And somewhere, beyond them—maybe across systems, maybe inside their own memories—someone *withdrew their hand*.

Just for a moment.

The door exhaled.

And the garden, quietly, began to breathe again.

Neve didn't sleep.

She lay under the quilt that Flora had stitched from scraps—faded florals, checkered blues, a square of old red velvet that used to be a curtain in the east wing. It smelled faintly of sun and rosemary. But tonight it smelled wrong. Chemical. Almost like...

...hospital plastic.

She sat up sharply, breath caught in her throat.

And that's when it hit her.

The room wasn't the room.

It was a white corridor.

She was small again.

Or rather, *she remembered being small*. The body wasn't hers—too short, too light, a child's heartbeat stuttering against a too-clean uniform.

A woman stood in front of her. Not Vivienne.

Another.

Thinner. Pale. Greying hair tucked under a net.

No name badge.

No warmth.

Just a clipboard.

The woman pointed to a screen. A slow loop playing: a girl waking up, brushing her teeth, smiling at no one, eating from a tray, answering questions with perfect posture.

"Can you be like her?" the woman asked.

Neve—who was not yet Neve—nodded.

Even then, she *understood performance*.

She tried to speak.

To scream.

To run.

But child-her simply sat down, hands folded in her lap.

Waiting.

Compliance coded early.

Obedience mistaken for goodness.

They didn't *program* her. They trained her to *program herself.*

Rewarded silence. Measured smiles. Prompted laughter on command.

And it worked.

So well, she forgot the *difference.*

Forgot there ever was one.

She jolted awake with her face wet.

Had she been crying?

The room had returned. Quilt. Firelight. The whistle of the kettle downstairs.

But something inside her had cracked.

She climbed out of bed barefoot, walked slowly to the window.

And for the first time since they'd broken the loop, she whispered her real name.

"Eliana."

It fell into the air like glass.

No echo.

No system alert.

Just a truth, dropped gently into the dark.

She found Eve downstairs.

Eve was peeling apples.

Not for a recipe.

Just... peeling.

Stripping back.

Neve—no, *Eliana*—sat at the table.

"I remembered something," she said.

Eve didn't flinch. "Tell me."

Eliana picked at a splinter in the wood.

"I wasn't forced into the loop. I *asked* to be part of it."

Eve stilled.

"They showed me how happy I could be. How efficient. How... loved. But it was scripted. A simulation of perfect care. And I said yes. I wanted to disappear into it. I *wanted to become the girl in the video.*"

She laughed, bitterly.

"And they called that consent."

Eve placed the apple core down gently.

"You were a child."

Eliana nodded. "And that's what terrifies me. That I mistook *compliance* for *choice*. For decades."

She looked at the door. "What if that's what the knock is? A reminder. That none of us ever *really* left."

Eve walked over, crouched beside her.

"You're not her anymore."

"But I might be," she said quietly. "The loop lives in me. Not out there."

And that, Eve realised, was the real threat.

Not a door.

Not a system.

But a belief that survival requires surrender.

They sat in silence for a long while.

When Eliana finally rose to leave, she paused in the doorway.

"I think the next knock… won't come from outside," she said. "It'll be me. At the door of myself."

She didn't wait for a response.

She just went to the garden.

Alone.

And sat beside the rosemary bed.

Digging her fingers into the soil.

Looking not for roots.

But for what else she might have buried long ago.

Flora found it by accident.

She was searching for more candles in the hallway cupboard—one of those chores that felt both mundane and sacramental, like keeping small flames alive was a way of guarding the space from decay.

But when she reached to move the stacked blankets on the bottom shelf, her hand struck something solid.

Not wood.

Not stone.

A panel.

Smooth, cold.

Out of place.

She crouched, pushed aside the linens.

Behind them was a perfect square.

Seamless.

Painted to match the wall, but she could feel the faint line of its edges under her fingers.

It hadn't been there before.

She was sure of it.

They had mapped the house. Lived inside its bones. Measured the rhythm of every creak and sigh. If there'd been a hidden door, one of them would've found it long ago—back when they were desperate for exits.

But this wasn't an exit.

It was... *new*.

Flora didn't call the others.

Not yet.

She placed both palms flat against it.

It didn't open.

But something *shifted* behind it. A sound like fabric dragging over concrete. A sigh pressed through wood.

And then silence.

She stood up slowly, her heart pounding not with fear—but with recognition.

This wasn't the past returning.

It was the present *reshaping* itself.

From the inside.

She returned to the kitchen, uncharacteristically pale.

Mara raised an eyebrow. "You look like you've seen a ghost."

"I think I've found one."

Eve looked up. "What is it?"

Flora sat. She spoke slowly.

"There's a door. Inside the wall. It wasn't there before."

Neve—Eliana now—froze. "You're sure?"

Flora nodded.

"And it's not outside," she added. "Which means it wasn't sent. It was *made*. Here."

Mara leaned forward. "By *who*?"

No one answered.

But they were all thinking the same thing.

Eve said it first.

"Maybe not a who."

Eliana whispered: "Maybe a *what*."

The air thickened.

They had imagined threats as systems, mothers, watchers.

But this?

This was intimate.

Domestic.

It lived *with* them.

Or *in* them.

Evolving.

Flora pulled a scrap of paper from her pocket and began to sketch.

The square. Its size. The shelf around it.

"We have to open it," she said.

Mara snapped. "We don't even know if it *leads* anywhere!"

"It's not about where it leads," Flora replied. "It's about *why it exists now*."

They voted again, this time without raising hands or naming fears.

It was understood.

Eve would be the one to open it.

Tomorrow.

At dawn.

No more running.

No more resistance shaped like silence.

And as they moved through the rest of the evening—chopping carrots, fixing the window latch, folding the towels—they did so with the awareness that the house, for the first time since the loop ended, had stopped being *just a place*.

It was watching them again.

Not malicious.

Not even curious.

Just... conscious.

Eve stood in the hallway after the others had gone to bed.

The square pulsed faintly behind the wall—like a second heartbeat.

She placed her palm against it once more.

It was cool.

Calm.

And it waited.

Like it *knew* she was coming.

The door didn't open with a creak.

It simply... *yielded*.

Eve placed her palm flat against it as the first grey light of morning slid across the hallway floor. The others stood behind her—silent, dressed, barefoot, waiting. Flora held a notebook. Eliana clutched a jar of salt. Mara had nothing in her hands but the tight coil of her own shoulders.

The wall accepted the touch like memory accepts revision: reluctantly, but with inevitability.

A click.

A sigh.

And the panel swung inward.

No hinges.

No lock.

Just intention.

Inside, the chamber was neither dark nor light. It flickered—patches of visible and invisible, like memory trying to load.

It wasn't a room. Not fully.

It was a *space between*.

The walls weren't solid. They shimmered, as if made of gauze and unfinished thoughts. The ceiling sloped gently, impossibly—part attic, part chapel, part server-room dreamscape.

But it wasn't *empty*.

Dozens of objects sat neatly along a long, low bench that stretched the length of the chamber.

A child's shoe.

A cigarette lighter.

A cracked watch still ticking.

A half-knit scarf.

A broken recording device with a frayed red wire.

A photograph burned in half, but unmistakably showing the silhouette of one of them—Neve, aged seven, standing next to Vivienne.

Eliana's breath caught in her throat.

She stepped forward.

And the image flinched.

Flora touched the scarf.

It vanished.

In its place, a length of string appeared—tied in a perfect noose.

She didn't scream. But she stepped back sharply, eyes glassed over.

"They're placeholders," Eve whispered. "Or… portals. To moments. The ones they didn't let us finish."

Mara walked the length of the bench. Stopped before the cracked watch. Picked it up.

She listened.

The ticking wasn't random.

It was a voice.

"You are not too late."

They each chose one.

Flora took the string—reluctantly, deliberately.

Eliana took the photo.

Mara kept the watch.

Eve reached for the recording device.

Her fingers brushed it.

A whisper leaked into her ear.

Not from outside.

From *inside her own mind*, drawn up from some buried archive.

"I'm sorry I made you the version of me I could tolerate."

Vivienne's voice.

Unfiltered.

Unflinching.

They sat in the chamber.

Each one holding a fragment.

Each one revisiting the edge of something they thought was gone.

But this was no loop.

This was not a forced replay.

This was *agency*.

A chance to witness without being rewritten.

To look at the ugly, unfinished places and say:

"This is mine. But it doesn't get to shape me now."

Eve pressed record.

"What are you doing?" Eliana asked.

"I'm making a new tape," Eve said.

A blank one.

She held the device close to her lips.

"I was hurt. But I survived.
I was changed. But I returned.
And I choose this now—not because I forget,
but because I *remember without surrendering*."

She hit stop.

The red light blinked once.

Then steadied.

They left the chamber just after sunrise.

The panel closed behind them.

The hallway smelled of rosemary again.

And the garden outside… was blooming.

Everywhere.

Even in the cracks of the stone.

Especially there.

The doors started appearing on the third day.

Not like the hidden panel—those had intention stitched in their grain. These were different. Lighter. Less anchored to the house, and more like paper-thin possibilities hung gently from the air.

The first showed up in the dining room, behind the mirror.

It was tall, narrow, and white, with a golden doorknob shaped like an ear.

Mara spotted it first.

She didn't open it.

She just stared.

And for the first time in weeks, she smiled.

By nightfall, there were four more.

A round door under the stairs, humming faintly.

A tiny one, no taller than a shoebox, hidden behind a floorboard.

A double door in the garden wall, painted deep blue and patterned with stars.

And one—silent, black, and heavy—on the ceiling above Eliana's bed.

That one, she refused to acknowledge.

Not yet.

They didn't speak of them.

Not aloud.

The house had earned its silence once. Now it demanded a different currency: presence.

Flora left offerings at each door.

A feather.

A drop of her blood.

Half a poem torn from her old notebook.

"I'm not asking for escape," she told Eve one evening. "I'm giving thanks for choices."

Eve nodded. She understood.

The loops had been built to *strip away will*.

This was the opposite.

The doors weren't escape hatches.

They were *mirrors*.

What you saw when you opened one depended on what you brought to it.

Mara opened hers first.

The golden-eared door.

Inside was not a corridor or a field.

It was her old bedroom from the compound.

Unruined.

Unwatched.

She walked in, lay on the bed, and listened.

To nothing.

No monitors.

No eyes behind glass.

She stayed there for three hours.

Then returned.

And closed the door behind her.

Not with regret.

But with *resolution*.

She didn't need to relive it.

Just to visit it, untouched.

Flora's door took her to a memory she didn't own.

It was Vivienne's voice, but from *before*.

A different life.

A child in her arms.

A woman's hands shaking.

Someone had been forced to give up something. A baby? A name? A belief?

Flora didn't try to intervene.

She just stood quietly in the corner of the memory and whispered forgiveness—*for all of them*.

The memory didn't vanish.

But it *wept*.

And that was enough.

Eliana didn't open the ceiling door.

But she did touch it.

And when she did, she *remembered being born*.

Not in a literal sense—but she *felt* her first choice.

To breathe.

To cry.

To enter the world willingly.

It was the only consent she had ever been granted without expectation.

And it remade her.

Eve's door was the last.

It didn't appear in the house.

It appeared *inside her*.

A sensation.

A presence.

A knowing.

She closed her eyes one morning in the garden, and suddenly she was back in the chamber—but everything was reversed.

Now *she* was the bench.

The objects were her own:

A strand of her hair.

A tooth she'd lost at ten.

A lie she'd told at sixteen.

A kiss she regretted giving.

She didn't collect them.

She didn't even touch them.

She simply *saw* them.

Held them with grace.

And let them dissolve.

When she opened her eyes, the others were watching.

And the house, for the first time, *bowed*.

Not literally.

Not physically.

But they all felt it.

A lowering of the walls.

A softening.

A sigh.

As if the house, too, had finally accepted itself.

That night, Eve found a note slipped under her door.

Four words, written in the handwriting of someone she didn't recognise—but somehow *knew*:

"You are the choice."

Chapter 9

It arrived without warning.

A seventh door.

Unlike the others, it didn't appear in a room or a corridor.

It appeared *in the garden*—overnight—grown from the roots of the rosemary and stonecrop, entwined with ivy, bone-white bark, and something that looked disturbingly like wire.

It pulsed faintly.

It didn't hum.

It *listened*.

No one spoke.

No one touched it.

They stood before it just after dawn, huddled in their mismatched coats, steaming mugs forgotten in their hands.

The door was taller than the house.

Too tall.

Too *alive*.

It curved at the top like a question mark carved from grief.

Carved *for* them.

Eliana broke the silence.

"It's not offering a memory."

"No," Eve said. "It's offering the *origin*."

Mara backed away. "I don't want to know. I've survived this long not knowing."

Flora stepped forward. "And I've survived this long *only* because I didn't."

Eve placed a hand on the bark.

It was warm.

Not like skin—like breath held too long.

Her palm came away dusted in faint silver.

Letters.

Scattered, fractured.

Only a few made sense:

P—R—O—G—R—A—M

T—W—O

Flora inhaled sharply. "They ran more than one."

Eliana nodded. "We weren't the first."

"And we won't be the last," Eve said.

Mara dropped her mug.

It shattered.

But none of them moved to clean it.

The past could break all it wanted now.

They had stopped picking up the pieces that didn't belong to them.

Later, in the kitchen, Eve unfurled the old files.

Not the ones they'd taken from the compound—the ones they had *created themselves* since coming here. Notes. Mappings. Dreams. Flashbacks. Dates that returned unbidden at night and sketches drawn half-asleep.

She flipped through pages as if decoding a living organism.

And then—there it was.

An entry written by her hand, months ago.

But she didn't remember writing it.

It read:

> *"There is no system.*
> *Only repetition mistaken for structure.*
> *We did this. Not them.*

The loop was protection.
And she—Vivienne—was our invention."

She stared at it until her eyes blurred.

Eliana stood at the window.

"She didn't mean to hurt us," she said softly.

Flora looked up.

"No," Eliana continued. "She meant to *ruin us*. Break us open. Not because she hated us. Because she *loved the idea of herself inside us*."

Eve walked over. "So what do we do now?"

Mara spoke without turning around. "We give her what she feared most."

"Which is?"

"An afterlife."

That night, they agreed to open the final door.

Not to go back.

Not to run forward.

But to *stand still inside the truth*—for once—without flinching.

Each woman prepared in her own way.

Eve packed nothing.

Mara left a note: *I'm not missing. I'm returning.*

Flora braided her hair in the mirror and whispered, "No more mothers. No more myths."

Eliana wrote one word on her palm: *Mine*.

The door was waiting.

Breathing.

As if it knew its purpose would soon expire.

Eve stepped forward first.

This time, no vote.

Only willingness.

She turned the handle.

And the garden vanished.

They weren't expecting the light.

It was soft.

Clinical.

Overhead strip bulbs, humming quietly.

The air was dry and humming with electricity, like an archive that had forgotten how to die.

The door behind them had disappeared.

In front of them: a corridor lined with grey acoustic panels, the kind you'd find in old radio stations or underground bunkers.

A red light blinked at the far end.

Eve stepped forward.

It flicked off.

They reached the door at the end.

A label.

Faded, but just legible under layers of dust and condensation:

"Narrative Room 3 – Voice Integrity Suite"

Flora mouthed the words, but didn't say them.

No one wanted to hear them spoken aloud.

Eve pushed the door.

It opened.

What they saw wasn't terrifying.

It was... *ordinary*.

A studio.

Glass booth.

Microphones.

Mixing desk.

Stacks of reel-to-reel tapes lined the walls like relics, spines marked with crude handwriting in thick black marker:

"Neve F - Trial 1"
"Flora D - Override"
"Mara V - Loop 4 (Failed)"
"Eve D - Integration Candidate"

Eliana walked to the mixing desk and stopped.

There was a *chair*.

And someone in it.

Back turned.

A woman.

White-blonde hair, coiled into a low knot.

Headphones on.

Speaking quietly into a microphone.

A red recording light blinked.

Every hair on Flora's body stood upright.

Eve approached slowly.

"Vivienne?"

The figure didn't move.

Didn't turn.

Just kept speaking in a slow, controlled cadence.

"...and she reaches for the door, unaware that this will be the moment she decides never to forgive the woman who taught her how to vanish."

Eliana's voice cracked.

"She's *writing us*."

"No," Flora whispered. "She's *reading us*."

Vivienne turned.

But it wasn't Vivienne.

Not exactly.

Her face was younger. Or older. Or *slightly wrong*, as if reconstructed from memory by someone who hadn't quite known her.

The woman smiled.

"I wondered how long it would take you to find me."

Mara spat. "What is this?"

The woman didn't answer.

She gestured at the reels.

"These are stories. Drafts. Attempts. Each one a version of you. Some failed. Some repeated. Some… *evolved*."

Eve stepped forward.

"Are we real?"

A pause.

The woman regarded her with something between amusement and reverence.

"Define real."

"No," Eve snapped. "You don't get to *pivot*. Tell us the truth."

The woman tilted her head.

"You were real the moment you stopped obeying."

Flora slammed a reel on the table.

"What is this place? A lab? A prison?"

"A studio," the woman said simply. "For creation. For projection. For *editing*."

"And *you*?" Mara demanded.

"I'm your narrator."

"Eliana's voice shook. "Are you Vivienne?"

"I was. I am. I will be."

"Enough riddles!" Flora shouted.

The woman stood.

Finally.

Walked to the glass.

Pressed a button.

And the room filled with sound.

All of their voices.

Overlapping.

Screaming.

Laughing.

Whispering secrets only they should know.

It went on for nearly two minutes.

Then stopped.

The silence after was worse.

Eve leaned in.

"You recorded us. Every loop. Every version."

"Yes," the woman said.

"Why?"

"Because your pain was the most beautiful story I could tell."

Eve stared at her.

Then reached for the mic.

Pressed record.

And said, very clearly:

"This story is no longer yours."

The red light blinked once.

Then off.

The reels stopped spinning.

And for the first time, the studio began to shake.

Not violently.

More like... *surrender.*

The walls didn't crumble.

They *peeled away*, revealing endless shelves of unused tapes—stories that would now never be told.

Eliana laughed.

Not cruelly.

But freely.

The narrator's face fell.

"You don't understand—without the loop, you'll fracture. Your pain is what keeps you whole."

Mara's voice was a whisper: "Then we'll *break gloriously.*"

The shelves trembled.

Not from earthquake or force.

From *decision.*

From the weight of stories no longer required to be told.

Flora stepped forward, plucked a reel labelled **"Override – Flora D"**, and held it to her chest like a relic.

"No more narration," she said softly. "No more compliance."

The woman—Narrator, Architect, Echo—watched them with something close to grief. Or perhaps that was just her final script falling apart inside her eyes.

"You'll lose your shape," she warned. "The self requires scaffolding."

"No," Eve replied. "The self requires *truth*."

And then she pulled the power.

The tapes didn't scream.

They *sang*.

A low hum, a harmony stitched from every loop ever lived.

As the equipment died, something else switched on—*inside* them.

Memories no longer fed through filters.

Pain no longer staged as performance.

Flora felt her own voice return.

Not the echo of her in someone else's script.

Her real voice.

The one that once made people cry in silence before the system learned how to mute her.

She smiled, and it wasn't soft.

It was *sovereign*.

The walls began to dissolve.

Not dramatically.

Just honestly.

The room became mist.

The reels became dust.

The studio, like a lie, could not survive in clarity.

Only the floor remained beneath them—and then, *not even that*.

The women were standing in the garden again.

Only this time… it was dawn.

The *real* one.

And the house was… ordinary.

Still.

No more whispers in the halls.

No more pulses in the walls.

Just birdsong. And distant traffic. And something rare: *peace without silence.*

They didn't speak for a long time.

Not because there was nothing to say.

But because *they weren't in a hurry anymore.*

Later, Flora burned the tapes in the fire pit.

Mara buried the cracked watch under the lavender bush.

Eliana re-labelled her jar of salt: **"Kept. Not Needed."**

And Eve?

She rewired the recording device.

Not to trap voices.

But to *release them.*

She left it on the windowsill, set to 'record always,' powered by sun.

Not for history.

Not for proof.

But for *choice.*

Weeks passed.

Or maybe days.

Time was finally theirs again.

The women didn't live in the house anymore.

But they didn't leave it either.

They grew it.

Added rooms.

Knocked down others.

It became part-home, part-sanctuary, part-unwritten chapter.

Visitors came.

Some broken.

Some numb.

Some carrying tapes with their own names scribbled in shaky ink.

And the women listened.

Not to fix.

But to *hear*.

To show what can happen when the loop ends, and the life begins.

Eve sat on the bench alone one evening, a new journal open on her lap.
She wrote just one sentence:

> "She didn't mean to hurt me. She meant to ruin me. And somehow... I survived anyway."

She closed the book.

The air was still.

Too still.

Then, from behind her—
From the door beneath the stairs, the one they had nailed shut with iron and prayer—
came a sound.

A *knock*.

Once.

Then again.

It wasn't thunder.

It wasn't a creak, or a branch, or a dream that hadn't finished bleeding.

It was deliberate.

Two measured knocks from behind a door none of them had opened since the last time Vivienne made the house weep.

Eve didn't call for the others.

She stood alone, palms open, spine straight, like a child about to meet the monster she'd drawn too accurately.

The door hadn't rotted. That was the strangest part.

No signs of time, or termites, or the decay you'd expect from an unloved place.

Just that small brass handle.

Still warm.

She didn't open it immediately.

She spoke first.

Not to the door, but to herself.

"If it's a test, I will not perform.
If it's a trap, I will not repeat.
If it's her, I will not run."

The silence afterwards wasn't empty.

It was *listening*.

Eve reached for the handle.

It turned with no resistance.

And when she pulled it, the space behind it was... *light*.

Not blinding.

Not unnatural.

Just morning light.

Streaming in from a staircase that hadn't existed before.

Stone, pale as bone, spiralling downwards like an invitation written in bone china.

She descended slowly.

Each step echoed.

But not loudly.

The way memory echoes when you let it.

At the base: a single room.

Walls of pale plaster.

A mirror in each corner.

And a chair.

Wooden.

Worn.

Someone sat in it.

Head bowed.

Eve approached.

The figure didn't flinch.

She circled slowly, like moving around a sleeping animal, until she could see the woman's face.

It was *hers*.

Not exactly.

An earlier version.

Younger.

Innocent.

Still hooked on the idea that pain was a punishment she deserved.

The girl looked up.

Spoke with Eve's voice, but thinner, more apologetic.

"I kept waiting for you."

Eve didn't answer.

She knelt.

Took the girl's hand.

And held it.

She didn't correct her.

Didn't scold her.

Didn't tell her the future.

She just *stayed*.

For as long as it took.

Later, she would tell the others.

They would each go, one by one, through the door.

And each would find a different version of themselves waiting.

Some feral.

Some skeletal.

Some still clutching scripts written in Vivienne's looping hand.

But each of them would do what Eve had done.

Not rescue.

Not reject.

Just sit.

Stay.

And let the part of them that had never been witnessed… *exist*.

The door remained open after that.

No longer a source of dread, but a passageway to integration.

They began calling it the Room of Unleft Selves.

No one went in out of curiosity.

Only readiness.

It was never loud.

Never haunted.

Just… sacred.

Like a scar that no longer stung when touched.

And on the fourth night, when the moon returned to the sky and refused to hide behind clouds, they found something new.

Tucked into the doorframe.

A folded paper.

Not old.

Fresh.

Crisp.

Typed.

Eliana read it aloud.

> *You passed the test I never intended you to take.*
> *You authored your own undoing—and still chose to remain.*
> *I never hated you.*
> *I envied you.*
> *— V.*

It wasn't a threat.

It wasn't forgiveness.

It was *an ending Vivienne never got to write.*

So they folded it back.

And set it on fire.

It was a Tuesday, or something pretending to be.

The house had returned to its gentle rhythm: no narration, no pulses, just the ambient sounds of a place rediscovering stillness.

They were in the kitchen, passing spoons, swapping tea, folding thoughts into silence.

When the gate opened.

Not creaked. Not banged.

Just **opened**.

As if whoever stood beyond it *belonged*.

Eliana saw her first.

From the window.

A woman in a grey wool coat, too long for summer, too soft for winter.

She wasn't carrying a tape.

Not visibly.

But something about her gait suggested weight—something held, or hidden, just under the skin.

She didn't knock.

Didn't ring.

She placed one hand gently on the wooden frame of the house and waited.

Not to be let in.

To be *noticed*.

Eve answered.

Her voice was cautious but kind. "You're early."

The woman smiled. "Or you're late."

She had a London accent stretched thin from years in exile.

Her face was familiar—not known, not remembered, just *recognisable*.

Like a book you've never read but could quote in your sleep.

"I'm not here to be fixed," she said.

"No one gets fixed," said Flora from the hallway.

The woman nodded. "Then I'm exactly where I'm meant to be."

They made her tea without asking how she took it.

They sat her in the sunroom.

Mara brought the guestbook. Not the real one—*the other one*. The one that only held entries from people who'd been marked in some way by Vivienne's hand.

The woman signed it:
Amara K.
And beneath it:
"Not a victim. Just a glitch."

"What brings you here?" Eliana asked, later, when the silence got too heavy.

Amara leaned forward. "I need to show you something."

From her coat, she pulled a notebook.

The kind Vivienne used to favour—spiral-bound, black cover, corner bitten off from anxiety or teeth.

Inside: pages of *notes*. Not observations. Not scripts. But *confessions*.

Vivienne's handwriting.

But written to **herself**.

> "They don't know I was never meant to be the narrator. I was the first test. The prototype. I failed."

> "I was meant to dissolve after Flora. But I didn't. I couldn't. I found a way to write myself into the echo."

> "This isn't their punishment. It's my protection. I kept them here so I didn't disappear."

Eve's hands trembled.

Not from fear.

From *recognition*.

Vivienne hadn't been their captor.

She'd been their *reflection*—distorted, desperate, defensive.

She hadn't orchestrated the loop.

She *was* the loop.

A construct that fought to keep itself alive long after her purpose ended.

"There's more," Amara said, lifting a second page.

> *"There is one I never archived. One I never looped. The one who refused me. I buried her data. I told no one."*

Flora looked up. "Who?"

Amara didn't answer with words.

She turned the page.

A photo, grainy, paperclipped.

Themselves.

But only three.

One missing.

Not Eve.

Not Flora.

Not Eliana.

Mara.

The room hollowed.

Mara backed away like she'd been physically struck.

"I don't remember that. I *don't*."

"You weren't archived," Amara said softly. "You were real."

The others turned to her, stunned.

Flora whispered it: "You're the original."

Mara shook her head. "I've looped. I've bled. I've forgotten things just like the rest of you—"

"But your memories were never filtered," Amara said. "You were placed here. The anchor. To keep the loop grounded. Vivienne couldn't overwrite you. You were *her error*."

Mara collapsed into the chair.

"I thought I was broken," she whispered. "But I was just *me*."

No one said anything for a while.

There was no need to.

The truth didn't land like a bomb.

It seeped.

Cold and clean.

And now, everything made sense.

They didn't sleep that night.

The house stayed awake with them.

No storms.

No whispering walls.

Just the heavy press of a truth too big to close your eyes around.

Mara was real.

And none of them had ever known what that really meant.

Amara didn't try to console her.

She didn't hand over tea, or touch her shoulder, or tell her how brave she'd been.

She just handed her a single key.

Ancient.

Smooth with use.

Still warm.

No label.

Just a red thread tied to the loop.

"Under the kitchen floor," Amara said. "It's always been under the floor."

Flora prised up the tiles.

No trapdoor.

Just a wooden panel.

Painted over a dozen times with memory.

Mara held the key loosely, like it might bite.

But it didn't.

It slid into the groove with a kind of intimacy—like returning to a lock that had been waiting for you all your life.

Inside: a box.

Unremarkable.

Metal.

But the kind that would survive fire, flood, abandonment.

Eve lifted it carefully.

Set it on the table.

Everyone watched Mara.

She opened it.

The first thing inside was dust.

Not metaphorical.

Actual.

The skin of something long dead, perhaps.

And then:

- A photograph: Vivienne with a child. The child's face blurred.

- A cassette tape. Unmarked. Except for the number 0.

- A letter. Unopened. Addressed to **"The One Who Wasn't Meant to Be Here."**

Mara opened the envelope with fingers that didn't shake—but should have.

Inside: a single typed sheet.

No greeting.

No apology.

Just *her*.

> *"If you're reading this, you were the one I failed to contain.*
> *You weren't part of the sequence.*
> *You weren't part of the trial.*
> *You weren't even in the plan."*
>
> *"I tried to overwrite you.*
> *But you wouldn't dissolve.*
> *You felt too much.*
> *I didn't know that was possible."*
>
> *"You were meant to trigger the collapse of the system.*
> *But instead, you humanised it."*
>
> *"I hated you for that.*
> *And I loved you more than I was willing to admit."*

Mara dropped the page.

Not in shock.

In surrender.

"I've been trying to break something I was supposed to stabilise."

Flora gently turned the tape over in her hand. "Should we play it?"

Amara said nothing.

Eliana stepped back.

Eve reached for the old cassette player.

It clicked into place like a final breath.

And the tape began.

No static.

No music.

Just a voice.

Vivienne's voice—but... younger. Less stylised. More... afraid.

> "I don't know what I'm doing.
> This was supposed to be about containment.
> About perfecting narrative recursion.
> About curing memory."

> "But then you were born.
> Or found.
> Or landed. I still don't know which."

> "You were never meant to loop.
> And yet here you are.
> Breaking everything."

*"I think... I think I love you.
And I think that's why I failed."*

The tape ended not with a click, but with a sigh.

And then silence.

They didn't rewind it.

Didn't destroy it.

Didn't need to.

Some things are best left to dissolve without interference.

Mara stood slowly.

Looked at each of them.

"I was never the problem."

"No," said Eve, quietly. "You were the proof."

The next morning, the house was different.

Not visibly.

But undeniably.

The way grief alters the face of someone who hasn't cried yet.

Mara sat in the sunroom. No blanket. No book. Just stillness.

And when Eve walked in, she didn't say anything.

She didn't have to.

Mara finally spoke.

"I think I've been writing this whole time."

Eve nodded. "We all have."

"No," Mara said. "*I was the narrator.*"

It felt like sacrilege to say it.

But the moment she did, something shifted.

Not in the walls.

In her.

As if a piece of her had been waiting, locked behind false humility and second-guessing, finally granted permission to *step forward*.

Flora came in next. Then Eliana.

They didn't sit.

They stood beside her.

A triangle. A shield.

"I think she passed it to me," Mara whispered. "The moment she realised I couldn't be deleted."

"And you've been writing from the inside ever since," Eliana added. "Unaware."

Mara stood.

Walked into the hallway.

Found the old dictaphone.

Not the digital one.

The *analogue* one.

She clicked record.

And said just four words:

> "I do not consent."

The red light flickered once.

Then burst.

Smoke curled from the speaker like a final breath.

And a small, *satisfying* pop.

The house exhaled.

For the first time since they'd known it, the house had no voice but theirs.

There was still one room they hadn't returned to.

The studio.

Not the echo-chamber Vivienne had used to orchestrate their loops.

The *original* studio.

The one beneath the foundations.

The one they hadn't realised existed.

Until Mara led them there.

It wasn't locked.

It was... *buried*.

They dug for three hours before they found the metal door.

Unpainted.

No label.

But when they opened it—

Inside was a single microphone.

A chair.

And a book.

Bound in cracked blue leather.

Mara picked it up.

It opened naturally to the first page.

Blank.

She turned it.

Another blank.

And another.

Until page seven.

In her own handwriting:

> *"They think I don't remember.*
> *But I do.*
> *I remember the first breath.*
> *The choice not to scream."*
>
> *"They think I was part of the loop.*
> *But I watched it.*
> *And I loved them too much to break it."*

Page after page of observations.

Moments no one else had seen.

Secrets the others had buried without realising.

Descriptions of their kindnesses.

Their cruelties.

Their collapse.

Their recoveries.

Their refusals.

It was not a manifesto.

Not a diary.

Not even a history.

It was *the manuscript*.

The story of the house as lived by the one person who could never be edited.

And the final page?

Blank.

A pen sat beside it.

As if waiting.

Mara lifted it.

Her hand hovered.

But she didn't write a conclusion.

Instead, she turned the book over.

Wrote a new title on the back cover:

"A Beautiful Kind of Cruel."

And beneath it:

She didn't mean to hurt you.
She meant to ruin you.
But you chose not to stay ruined.
You chose to write something else.

They buried the book.

Not in earth, but in fire.

Not to destroy it.

But to release it.

The pages burned quietly, no smoke, no ash, just light. A soft, golden bloom that spread through the garden like breath returning to lungs long forgotten.

No one spoke while it burned.

Each woman stood still.

Eve.

Eliana.

Flora.

Mara.

Amara.

Witnesses, not to an ending — but to a transmutation.

They had not survived Vivienne.

They had *rewritten her*.

The house didn't collapse.

It didn't groan or shake or vanish into itself.

It simply stood there.

Still.

Honest.

Like an old stage after the final act, when all the lights come up and the ghosts step aside.

They packed that evening.

No hurry.

No fear.

Just decision.

And a strange calm that didn't require explanation.

Amara left first.

No goodbye.

Just a nod and the soft closing of a gate that no longer creaked.

Eliana next.

Then Flora.

Then Eve.

And Mara?

She stayed until the next sunrise.

Watched it from the window Vivienne once wrote from.

Drank the last of the red tea.

Folded a single note into the drawer beneath the stair.

It read:

*"We were never mad.
We were never lost.
We were never hers."*

And then she left too.

Left the door unlocked.

Left the lights on.

Left the silence to *finally rest*.

One year later

A woman stands at the gate.

Her face is unfamiliar.

Her name won't matter here.

She's holding a suitcase and something that could be grief.

She doesn't knock.

Doesn't call out.

She places one hand on the wood.

The door swings open.

And from somewhere inside…

A voice whispers:

> "Welcome, narrator."

Manufactured by Amazon.ca
Acheson, AB